THE CONNECTICUT COWBOY
And
THE RUNAWAY BRIDE

A Romantic Comedy

By Patricia Costa Viglucci

THE CONNECTICUT COWBOY
AND
THE RUNAWAY BRIDE©

Published by Stone Pine Books,
An imprint of Patri Publications
Rochester, NY
Copyright 1991, 2011, 2015
Patricia Costa Viglucci
patcosta@rochester.rr.com
Cover Photo of Portofino© by Johanna Bartlett, April 2014
Cover Design by Austin Bartlett

When Caitlin Harris's fiancé, an insurance executive, delays their wedding and honeymoon for the third time, Cait throws down her engagement ring and takes off for the Italian and French Rivieras on her own. At her first stop in enchanting Portofino, she encounters Jake Riordan, an urbane New Englander, whose sophisticated look clashes with his western footgear. Clearly he's no cowboy, but there's more to him than meets the eye. When her rental car is damaged, Cait reluctantly takes up Jake's offer to share her hotel suites for the rest of the trip in exchange for transportation.

His luxurious Mercedes takes them to Monaco, Monte Carlo, Nice and the gorgeous Italian Lakes, Como and Maggiore. Cait fights her attraction for Jake when he tells her about a girl back home. A drive to the beautiful resort of Bellagio on Lake Como and a near dunking in the lake, resulting in the forced sharing of accommodations in an Italian mountain cottage, brings things to a head.

Author's Note: Years ago, my husband and I with our three children traveled the same magical itinerary as do Caitlin and Jake in this story--from Portofino on the Italian Riviera to Monaco and Nice on the Cote D'Azur. From there we traveled to Milan, then to the city of Como and to Cernobbio where our comfortable hotel faced Lake Como and the opposite mountain, lit at night with "twinkling fairy lamps." We also took a scary drive around Lago di Como to the magnificent resort of Bellagio, the nail-biting details which inspired an important part of this novel. (Stresa on Lake Maggiore was a later trip, but I worked it into this story.)

I knew the trip would make a wonderful backdrop for a romantic tale. Thus this novel. Technology was hardly up to today's speed. I chose to leave it as originally written without cell phones, internet or other such devices.
**

PROLOGUE

The smell of fresh paint filled the office of the small elegant hotel just off the Via Veneto. Hammering from the adjacent lobby added to the assault on the senses as workmen hung paintings of ethereal muses ala Botticelli, and a tapestry fragment reputed to be from the Medici looms.

Jake Riordan was oblivious to such minor distractions, his attention on his long-time friend, Paolo Cimino, the owner of the newly refurbished establishment.

A moment before, Reception had alerted Paolo, informing him there was an incoming call from the states.

"Aramis!" Paolo clutched the receiver, dredging up the old nickname in his excitement. "Is it really you?"

Jake's eyebrows rose. His look mirrored the amazement in Paolo's dark eyes. It had been years since either man had been in touch with their former Yale suitemate. That he should call Paolo during Jake's visit to Rome was an extraordinary coincidence.

Jake gathered that the call was something about a woman. Of course.

As Jake watched, Paolo's expressive countenance underwent startling transformation.

"What!" Paolo bellowed into the receiver, his Italian sense of fitness clearly assaulted. "My God, man, how could you let such a thing happen? If she's the innocent you say she is, she could be in danger!"

Jake frowned. Now what? Seeing Jake's mystified look, Paolo motioned for him to pick up an extension.

Jake listened in silence for several moments, shaking his head in disbelief as he met Paolo's glance. Putting down the phone, he studied the tips of his western boots from under half-closed lids.

Aramis. The schemer and politician. A leftover from freshman year theatricals, the name fit their friend. This time, however, his machinations had worked against him. His lady love might not be a sophisticate, but apparently she possessed an independent streak.

Paolo was doing his best to soothe the caller. "I'll do whatever I can. Listen! Riordan is here. He flew in yesterday to help me celebrate the reopening of the hotel. He'll want to help."

Jake swore softly. Now he was in for it.

Paolo continued, "I agree, it can't be done by phone. One of us will go check on her. Don't worry. Nothing could have happened in such a short time."

Jake's snort spoke volumes. Paolo never turned his back on anyone he considered a friend, his generosity legendary. Jake waited until the Italian ended the overseas call then expressed himself in a few explosive words.

Paolo shrugged elegant Armani-clad shoulders and reached for a pen. "What was I to do? I couldn't just let the guy hang."

"I would have. We put an end to the Three Musketeers rubbish long ago." Jake stared upward, his gaze tracing the arches of the freshly painted frieze. "Looks like the Smooth Operator has finally managed to screw up in a colossal way."

"I never heard him in such a stew. It was the last place he expected any opposition. I'm guessing that up to now, she's been putty in his hands." Paolo chuckled, doodling on the new desk pad. "I told him I'd go take a look and assess the situation."

"How in blazes are you going to go?" Jake shot a look at his friend. "Your grand opening is the day after tomorrow. You're needed here."

"I gave my word, Jake."

Jake knew when he was licked. Paolo was loyal to a fault. "No, I'll go," he growled. Jake gestured, taking in the smart, tasteful surroundings. "A fine grand opening it would be without you."

Paolo grasped at the offer. "You can take my car. Soak up some sun. Take time to unwind." The Italian's dark gaze softened as he came around the desk, hand outstretched. "You're a good friend, Jake. You always were—to both of us."

Jake got to his feet, jabbed his friend in the shoulder. "Let's get one thing straight, pal. I'm doing this for you, for Paolo Cimino. Not for that bleepin' blockhead."

Chapter I

From the third floor balcony of her room at the Hotel Fiorito, Caitlin Harris stared glumly at the sparkling blue of the Ligurian Sea.

Its sapphire depths, combined with the sweet drifting scent of oleander, underscored her single state and filled her with longing.

Portofino was a spot that travel posters could only hint at, a true paradise with its mix of pine trees and palms, verdant hills dotted with grand villas, and best of all, the silken caress of warm air on face and bare arms. Perfect for lovers.

"So what kind of idiot comes to such a place alone?" she muttered.

It was a question Caitlin had asked herself a dozen times since last night's arrival at the former villa nestled on the hillside. It would have been far better if she'd gone to Rome or Florence where she would have blended into the crowds.

No. She shook her head setting dark gold tendrils in motion. She mustn't think like that. She was a new woman, ready to cope with whatever happened. She proved that 72 hours ago. Caitlin closed her eyes for a moment to exorcise any lingering doubts, the early morning breeze off the sea whipping at the ties of her filmy negligee.

She had been dreaming of this Riviera trip for years, ever since her grandfather had brought home a jigsaw puzzle of the small, enchanting Italian port. As a young man he had seen naval duty in this verdant part of the world, and the memory of its lush magnificence never left him.

Caitlin, an imaginative twelve-year-old, was fascinated first by his stories and then the puzzle as it took shape. The completed picture cast a permanent spell upon her, the yachts and small fishing boats lying side by side in the narrow inlet, pastel houses climbing up the rocky incline. She vowed then that some day she would see it for herself.

Had she listened to Daniel, Caitlin mused, she would have been cheated out of all this. As it was she'd paid a steep price for realizing this particular fantasy.

Caitlin's gaze dropped to bare tapering fingers. Was it really only days since she'd slid the outsized diamond ring from her hand and dropped it on Daniel's desk? She'd never warmed to the expensive chunk of ice, a gaudy substitute for the pearl in the antique setting she favored. Daniel's sneer made it clear the modest ring would be a poor reflection on a man of his standing and considerable wealth, a man who would be able to fulfill her every material dream. But as Caitlin had reflected then and now, there was more to life than material riches.

Still Caitlin found it hard to believe that she'd turned her back on the future Daniel had planned for them.

The sound of footsteps on the gravel below broke into her thoughts. Opening her eyes, she spotted a long white yacht in the distance, then for the first time glanced down into the narrow road that ran between sea and hotel. Below, stood a man staring up at her.

An urbane figure, whose tailored clothes fit the rangy frame with careless perfection, he exuded sophistication. That is, he did until Caitlin's gaze, traveling downward, reached the pointed footwear. She frowned. What kind of person wore cowboy boots to the Riviera?

Her gaze flitted back up the lean, tall figure to the bronzed face. He was still staring, eyes glinting, mouth curved. He nodded to her.

Churlish not to respond, but her return nod was barely perceptible, and the smile he flashed back mocked her compressed lips.

His eyes, the color of the sapphire sea behind him, were intent upon her. "Lovely view," he said, his voice carrying clearly.

"Glorious," she started to reply, when some instinct made her aware he was not referring to the body of water. She looked down, embarrassment rooting her to the spot. The breeze had whipped open the ties of her negligee to expose an expanse of apricot silk and even greater span of pale skin.

Sucking in air, she clutched the edges of the filmy wrap and willing her feet to obey, backed through the open French doors to her room. An unsettling laugh floated upward.

In the wavy cheval mirror she glimpsed herself, the reflection deepening her color. The gossamer nightgown was one of several she had bought for her bridegroom's edification. Like the others, it left little to the imagination.

She closed the French doors, trembling with anger. It had been a mistake to come. Her younger sister Liz had warned her.

"Go alone on what was to be your honeymoon? You're crazy, Caitlin! What does Daniel say to this plan of yours?"

"He thinks I'm bluffing," she said, then added reluctantly, knowing full well the effect her words would have on her sister. " I gave him back his ring."

Liz, 24, married and the mother of six-month-old Jessica, stared at Caitlin. "You've broken off with Daniel Sloane? You *are* crazy! Three years out of your life and you're tossing it away?"

Caitlin stood her ground. "He'd already postponed the wedding twice before."

"What did he say when you called it off?" Liz persisted.

"Not much." Actually Daniel had given her that superior smile, the one that implied she was 16 instead of 26, and asked, "Do you know what you are doing, Caitlin?"

It had been that smug question which had convinced her. That and the look on his face. Daniel was too well bred to smirk, but his expression of long suffering patience blended with amusement had come close, pushing Caitlin over the edge.

Without hesitating, she slid off the outsized rock and walked out, ignoring his parting shot that without him she wouldn't last three days and would come "tearing home."

Caitlin knew it was Daniel's belief that he had quelled her rebellion which kept him from calling. He was waiting until she came crawling back, all apologies for presuming to think for herself. After three years, Caitlin knew how Daniel's brain worked.

It was the mechanics of her own mind which sometimes puzzled her. Liz had pressed her, obviously trying to fathom Caitlin's reasons for throwing away a catch of Daniel's stature. *"What is it you want, anyway, Caitlin?"*

At an early age, her sister Liz had just want Liz wanted, including a husband who adored her, *and* darling Baby Jessica.

Caitlin stared unseeing at the Fiorito's sprigged wallpaper. What *did* she, Caitlin, want? Nothing so extraordinary. Someone who would put her first, before business, before his other interests.

Someone whose face would light up every time she came into the room, who would find excuses to touch her, to drop a kiss on the top of her head and a few other places.

The early excitement in their relationship had dissipated almost at once, Caitlin reflected, as Daniel, absolutely sure of her, focused on preparing her to be the perfect executive wife. In his headlong rush to mold her to his specifications, he seemed hell-bent on eradicating those very things which had initially attracted him.

The qualities which made Caitlin Caitlin included her penchant for old treasures, particularly fabrics, and her work of restoring them. There was little monetary reward in such an occupation and the great satisfaction she derived from saving a client's generations-old quilt or heirloom christening dress was of no consequence to her former fiancé. If one's work didn't lead to financial gains, it was not a worthy pursuit. Even a Christmas Eve family gathering Daniel promised to attend gave way to a dinner with some hot prospects.

Strangely enough, only Liz had questioned Caitlin's motives in telling Daniel goodbye. Her parents, no doubt remembering the less biddable, independent young woman Caitlin had been in the pre-Daniel years, quietly accepted her decision to break off with him.

Gran, alone, cheered her on. "Serves him right, Cait darlin'. You deserve better than that so and so," she said lapsing into the salty language that she'd picked up from her sailor husband and which so offended the proper Daniel. Caitlin grinned, remembering how Daniel and her grandmother had been hard pressed to remain civil to each other. Looking back, it did seem as if she had been under some kind of spell. Initially, Caitlin was awed by Daniel's take-charge manner. In the end, however, it was his dogmatic ways which caused her to rebel.

The rumblings of her stomach halted her reflections. The Fiorito's dining room had been closed when she had arrived last night, and she had made do with a package of crackers and a miniature wedge of foil-wrapped cheese left from the train ride from Genoa.

Showering in the yellow-tiled bathroom which connected with another bedroom, she wondered what Daniel's opinion would have been on sharing facilities with strangers. Of course, had Daniel deigned to come, they would have used the connecting bedroom themselves.

Unbeknownst to Caitlin, Daniel had instructed Ingrid, his efficient (and adoring) secretary, to upgrade the one room Caitlin had reserved at each hotel to either a suite or two connecting rooms. The other room in each case was to be used as an office so as not to keep Caitlin "awake at night."

Caitlin attempted to change the reservations before she took off by herself, but time was against her. When she arrived at the Fiorito alone, however, the management, citing heavy holiday bookings, was glad to take the extra room off her hands.

Caitlin was relieved. Besides being a waste, it would have been still another reminder that Daniel did not think her important enough, or more to the point, desirable enough, to put aside his all-consuming work for two weeks.

In the bedroom Caitlin chose an outfit and dressed, then stopped in front of the wavy mirror to assess herself.

If Daniel's cavalier treatment had done nothing for her self-esteem, the cowboy's frank appraisal, as honest as it was disturbing, had done much to offset the negative feelings.

And when she finally made her way down to the first floor the dining room occupants confirmed the cowboy's assessment. A table of university students on Spring break ogled her, one of them commenting in Italian on her figure.

Ignoring them, Caitlin followed Marisa to the breakfast room overlooking the sea. The owner's teenage daughter showed her to a small table and Caitlin expressed pleasure in the small nosegay centered on the white cloth, lifting the miniature vase to breathe in the fragrance. "*Bella,*" she murmured. "Beautiful."

Run by Signora DeLuca and assorted female relatives, the converted villa had only 20 bedrooms. Long on charm and comfort, short on luxury, unless you counted the scenery, it was Caitlin's idea of the perfect lodging. Daniel had opted for the luxury hotel on top the mountain, and it had taken some doing for her to convince him that the Fiorito would be up to his standards.

Caitlin smiled at the waiting Marisa. "*Caffe latte per favore,*" she requested and the young girl quickly brought silver pots of steaming coffee and hot milk. She alternated pouring them into

Caitlin's cup, returning to the antique sideboard for a basket of still warm *panini*. The hollow, crusty rolls begged for a dollop of *marmellata*.

Caitlin took one, relishing the aroma, and put it on her plate, then took a sip of the very strong coffee. Quickly she added sugar to offset the potency. Usually, she drank her coffee black but this was a delicious brew unlike any at home.

Caitlin was making short work of the delectable roll when the sight of Marisa approaching once more caught her attention.

Behind the girl was... the *cowboy*, still dressed in the tailored jacket and slacks. Without thinking, Caitlin glanced at his feet, then to his face, grimacing as she thought of the view she had afforded him a short while before. He gave her a bland smile, his teeth white in the tanned face.

"Please, Signorina," began Marisa, who then pointed out in rapid Italian that the dining room was full, and would Caitlin mind, just this once, if the gentleman, also American, shared her table.

Caitlin glanced around the room. It *was* crowded. She was inclined to accommodate Marisa when she saw the cowboy's smile.

"I'm sorry, but," she began when the scraping of the chair legs against the wood floor drowned out her words. Before she could close her mouth, the cowboy sat opposite her.

"Very nice of you," he murmured with pseudo politeness. Caitlin's back stiffened. No sense in making a fuss in the compact room. Pointedly, she picked up a travel book she had brought with her and turned to the section marked Liguria.

She read two paragraphs registering nothing, her mind on the very male, very virile presence opposite her. Wide shoulders blocked the view behind him and glossy brown hair, the color of Italian chestnuts, was thick and luxurious. Silently, she listened as he attempted to give his order in phrase-book Italian.

Marisa was becoming confused, then embarrassed. "Please, Signore?"

He repeated the mangled words and Caitlin suppressed a smile. Served him right. With any luck he'd end up with squid for breakfast. Her college Italian honed with the help of Antonietta, the Tuscan-born seamstress who worked at Caitlin's shop, was at least serviceable.

Marisa, mindful that even more people were entering the breakfast room, was becoming agitated. Taking pity on the little waitress, Caitlin put down her book, and in precise Italian, relayed his order: melon, a large orange juice, two eggs sautéed lightly in olive oil, a pot of coffee.

"Ahh, ahh," cried Marisa, all gratitude. "*Grazie, Signorina*," she said smiling and scurried off to the kitchen. The cowboy, his face a blank, surveyed Caitlin. "Thank you, Ma'am."

Texan? Caitlin rejected the idea out of hand, nodded coolly and went back to her book.

"Connecticut," he said, reading her mind, "born and bred."

"Oh?" She looked at him suspiciously.

"And you?" The western drawl had disappeared, his words clipped.

"Hartford," she said reluctantly not wanting to divulge any information about herself to this man.

"What! Not a fellow nutmeg?" His look mocked her. He studied her, letting his gaze travel over her outfit. "Of course, you're in insurance."

Caitlin stiffened, only half-aware she was rubbing her ring finger. "Why do you say that?"

"Hartford's the insurance capital of the U.S." His gaze went over her again taking in the nondescript white blouse, the navy skirt, the hair confined at her nape with a barrette. "The uh...solid look you convey."

Caitlin cringed. Dowdy, he meant. She blamed herself for heeding the travel book, which had touted wrinkle-free clothes and comfortable shoes as wardrobe mainstays.

"By that token," she murmured, "You must be a cowboy. A Connecticut cowboy."

His laughter rang out, warm and deep-timbered, drawing glances. Caitlin, who hated being the center of attention, withdrew behind her travel book, wishing with all her heart she had gone into the village for coffee."

"So you noticed the boots?"

"They're hard to miss," she said without looking up.

"I've a Stetson in the car."

"Exhibitionist," she muttered under her breath. She stared at him. His reserved, cosmopolitan air didn't reach to his eyes. They were dancing, offering mute testimony to his enjoyment. She stuck her shapely nose further into her book.

Marisa's arrival with more coffee and steaming milk broke the silence. Caitlin waited for the cowboy to lift his cup, but instead he stuck out a lean hand across the table. "I'm Jake Riordan. From West Haven.

Caitlin hesitated, then put out her hand and let him enfold it in the warmth of his large, tanned one. Her heart thudding, it took her a moment to realize he was waiting for her name.

Annoyed at the effect he was having on her, she pulled her hand away, mumbling, "Caitlin. Caitlin Harris."

"Ah, Caitlin." He rolled it around on his tongue, as if it were fine wine. "I like it. Lots of young girls named Caitlin these days, but not too many your age. She shot him a glance, decided not to take umbrage at the reference to her advanced years.

Caitlin looked up into the very blue eyes, then averted her gaze as she felt herself drowning, only half-aware she was moving the non-existent engagement ring up and down on her finger.

"Leave your husband or boyfriend at home?"

"What!" She followed his gaze and tore her hands apart. "Neither!"

"Must have been a boyfriend." He took a sip of the strong coffee and milk mixture he had served himself. "You don't look married."

"And you don't know how to mind your own business!" She picked up the travel book and thrust it high in front of her to block out his face. The white blouse rose and fell as shallow breaths belied her calm exterior.

"You've dunked your book in the marmalade." Jake plucked the book from her unresisting fingers and made a big show of wiping it off with his napkin. Caitlin looked down her shapely nose at him. There was no marmalade on the snowy white linen; there had been none on the book.

The arrival of Marisa stilled her retort. The waitress, in spite of Caitlin's careful enunciation, had bungled the order. She had brought two of everything, including the olive oil eggs. She placed one in front of Jake, the other before Caitlin.

"But, I didn't…" Caitlin began.

"Shh," whispered Jake, as if they were conspirators. "She might cry if you tell her it's not right," and smiling, he waved the little waitress away.

Glaring at Jake, Caitlin picked up a fork and took a tentative bite of the eggs.

Surprise showed on her face. "They're very good…"

Jake was eyeing her with satisfaction. "We've a chef straight from Caserta at our Providence inn. He always fixes them for me this way."

You're in the hotel business?" The question slipped out before she could stop herself.

"Country inns. Here and there on the East Coast and our most recent acquisition in Texas. Realization dawned. The western boots and the Stetson.

Again he read her mind. "They were gifts from the staff at the Texarkana House. They bet me I wouldn't have the nerve to wear them in Europe." His gaze slid slyly over her face. "Sorry to disappoint you."

She fumed inwardly at the on-target assessment. "I never gave it a thought."

His smile was calculated to infuriate. "Of course you didn't."

Caitlin gave him a look and then turned back to her breakfast.

"Are you staying in Portofino long?"

"A couple of days."

"And, then?"

In her attempt to shut him up, she again proved indiscreet. "Up the Cote D'Azur, brief stop in Monaco, a couple of nights in Nice, Italian Lake District."

No Italian cities?"

"Just an overnight in Milan." Daniel had nixed "the church and museum trail" as he dubbed it and she had given in. Caitlin had promised herself a return visit to Rome and Florence to explore among other gems, the Vatican's tapestry gallery and the Uffizi's treasures.

Jake toyed with his cup. "A romantic itinerary. And you're traveling alone. I know American women are independent, but…."

"I don't see any problem. I can handle a car and I can read a map. No special feats."

"Still, I suspect your boyfriend must have had some objections to your traveling solo. It's not always safe over here for unescorted women. And the Europeans drive like crazy men—over 100 miles an hour on the Autostrada."

Caitlin frowned. "I can handle it." Men were all alike, always underestimating women's ability to take care of themselves. She bit down on her lower lip, a gesture that drew his attention.

"This trip…." He played with his spoon, tapping it gently against his cup, "…sounds almost like a wedding trip. Alluring, exotic, out-of-the-way places."

Anger surged through her. It was none of his business…

"It was, wasn't it?"

She sat stony-faced, paralyzed, a doe caught in the headlights of his stare.

"Backed out, did he?"

"No!"

"You did then?"

"No!" Afterward she would wonder why she had not simply stood up and stalked out. But her legs refused to move. "Neither of us did. He had to work. A conference. He'd already postponed the trip twice before. I was tired of waiting." She broke off, furious with herself for revealing any information to him.

"I can't imagine any conference taking precedence over a honeymoon with a beautiful bride." Jake looked at her. "Maybe his job was at stake?"

Caitlin's sorely tried heart rose with the compliment. "No, he's the boss. He called the conference."

"Oh." Jake's tone was not admiring. His long, studied survey made her forget Daniel, the dining room, everything but the two of them. Caitlin swallowed her reaction to Jake's scrutiny which was as unnerving as the conversation she had permitted to take place.

To Caitlin's gratitude, when Jake spoke it was to change the subject. "Strangely enough, I happen to be following much the same itinerary, or rather I had planned to. I didn't make hotel reservations…. soon enough. The Easter season is always busy and I was lucky to get in at the Fiorito. A friend in Rome who lent me his car knows Signora DeLuca. Otherwise I'd have been holed up in the city for the duration of my stay."

"Hardly a deprivation."

"No, but then I'd come with the purpose of visiting small hotels in this area. I was detoured by an unexpected errand, which has been…taken care of. Our group is seriously considering the possibility of acquiring one or two properties in out of the way tourist locations, away from the large cities.

He gave Caitlin a searching look, which made her wonder if she'd missed something. But the smile that followed dispelled the thought.

"Our guests sometimes ask us to recommend lodgings over here that approximate the kind of service and ambiance we offer," Jake continued. "Such an expansion seems like a natural. Friendly, low-key spots."

Caitlin nodded. It was why she had chosen the Fiorito and the other hotels, preferring small, family-run operations to the big impersonal ones.

He shot her another look. "You didn't change reservations after you found you were traveling alone? You should have invited a relative or girlfriend to accompany you."

"Why?" Not that it was any of his business, but there hadn't been time. Not that Liz would have left the baby anyway, and Caitlin couldn't think of anyone else to whom she cared to explain her solo trip.

Jake studied her for a moment, his gaze moving to her shapely figure, then back to her face. "It's not the same here as traveling at home. Some Europeans think a woman on her own, particularly an American, is fair game, and are anything but subtle in pressing their attentions. It may not be as safe as you think." He paused, once more scrutinizing her as if she were a road map. "Especially if you are careless."

"I'm not!"

His look this time was not indulgent. "You think standing on a balcony in a bit of transparent silk is wise?" His voice turned dangerously flat. . "Or maybe," he drawled, "it was deliberate. Single girl, all alone, missing her man…"

Even as he had begun to speak, Caitlin could feel her face drain of color, then flame. Damn his impudence. Grabbing her handbag and book, she stood up, fire sparking from her gray-green eyes, disgust with herself for opening up at all, loathing this stranger for making her feel like a tart.

Without a backward glance, she swept through the breakfast room, head high, no evidence of the humiliation, which left her weak-kneed and threatened to land her on her face.

The breeze from the sea cooled Caitlin's hot face as she moved quickly outdoors and down the curving stone steps to the miniscule parking lot. Thank God for the Lancia. Backing the new model out carefully she headed toward the village of Portofino, less than a mile away. If anything could take her mind off that despicable man, Portofino could.

A hamlet of less than a thousand residents, the village proper restricted cars to its upper end, and visitors walked down to the water along a narrow street lined with picturesque shops and restaurants. The view at the end of the street was even better than the jigsaw puzzle. She drew in her breath with pleasure almost forgetting Jake Riordan.

The huge yacht she had seen earlier from her balcony was docked, its blue and white Greek flag flying. In the middle of the square, swarthy-faced old men were piling firewood. Signora DeLuca had told Caitlin the night before that a festival honoring San Giorgio, patron saint of the local church just off the piazza, was held April 23 to mark his feast day. There would be a parade and later a bonfire. Nearby some fishermen scraped down a small boat.

Caitlin walked along the streets that jutted out on either side of the inlet, tall narrow buildings painted in seeming haphazard fashion to glorious effect in shades of red and yellow. Peering in the first floor shop windows full of souvenirs she stopped at the sight of the familiar Kodak sign to purchase a one-use camera , tucking it in her purse for later. Here and there were outdoor booths where women were displaying handmade lace, a specialty of the region. Stopping at one, she examined a piece carefully, recalling she had worked on a similar item the year before. An ornamental bureau scarf, it had been old, not new like this, but the patterns were remarkably similar.

"*Squisito,*" Caitlin told the ancient woman who returned her smile." *Squisito*, Exquisite!" The flash of white teeth in the sun-weathered face, as lined as the fishermen's, lifted her spirits.

The stroll was also helping. Much of Caitlin's anger had evaporated, though she could not eradicate the sting of the cowboy's insult. Nor could she rid herself of feeling too much on her own. A small outdoor café in the middle of the piazza beckoned, so she sat down and when a white-coated waiter appeared ordered a cappuccino.

Savoring the blend of coffee and milk whipped to a creamy froth, she took in the view. Green hills, blue water and centuries-old architecture including a small castle blended into a panorama of breathtaking quality.

Had Daniel come, they would have been husband and wife, one mind, joined together, starting married life in the most romantic of settings.

But he had not come, had not though her important enough. Her mind leaped to Jake. She guessed he was Daniel's age, 33, or so. But Daniel, maybe by virtue of his work—insurance was a serious business—had already taken on the characteristics of his father—staid, conservative, overly protective, especially of her.

Well, better than implying she was a tramp, or worse, as Jake Riordan had. She sipped at the cappuccino, dwelling anew on the scene in the dining room, wishing that she had hurled some crushing invective before she fled.

Her repertoire of insults was inadequate, she decided with a shaky laugh when the approach of a figure made her look up. Caitlin drew in her breath and started to rise, but Jake Riordan pressed her gently back into her seat, his hand warm and disturbing on her shoulder.

"Don't go," he said quietly, "I want to apologize."

"It's not necessary," she muttered, torn between the hurt he had inflicted a short time before and the comfort of seeing a familiar face, even it were this man's.

"But it is. Very definitely." Jake looked down into her face, letting go of her shoulder to capture her fingers. "I knew, even when I said it, that you weren't the kind to flaunt yourself."

"Then why did you?" She quickly pulled her fingers from his, his touch unwelcome.

He shrugged. "Put it down to the demon in me I suppose. Or the fact that it could have been some other man getting an eyeful." His tone made it clear that such an event would have been far worse.

He searched her face, asked quietly, "Am I forgiven?"

Caitlin turned away from him. "There's nothing to forgive." She rose and Jake blocked her escape.

"You're still angry."

"I am not!"

Her denial, ridiculous in light of her tone, brought an unholy gleam to his eyes, but all he said was "Good," and suggested that they walk around together. Perhaps she would help him pick out some of the lace pieces for his mother and assorted female employees.

"I can't tell which items are women's headwear and which are tablecloths." Jake smiled at her, a ploy that was patently unfair, the gleam of white even teeth in the tanned face adding to his magnetism. She swallowed hard.

A fierce debate was taking place within her. The temptation to accompany this man with the sea blue eyes was great. Portofino was a place to wander *with* someone. Caitlin stopped herself just in time.

Avoiding his gaze, she murmured "Sorry," and added something about having other plans.

Jake smiled down at her, a friendly smile. For a moment she thought he was going to attempt to change her mind.

Instead, she heard, "I'm sorry, too." And before she had time to answer, his tall frame was lost in the crowd of day tourists who spilled out of the tour buses from Milan and were filling the narrow street.

Suddenly bereft, Caitlin moved aimlessly up the sloped walk, ignoring a postcard kiosk she had meant to investigate. She couldn't be lonely already. But, the charm had gone out of the setting and the day.

She drove back past the miniscule parking lot below the Fiorito and on toward San Margherita and saw her hotel's bathing beach on the right. She didn't feel like sunning herself, but then for some reason nothing else held much appeal either. She'd save exploring San Margherita for later.

Back in her room she donned a swim suit, a conservative one-piece navy, and slipped a skirt and blouse over it. Grabbing a towel and a book, she made her way back to the small parking lot, then drove the short distance to the beach. She could have walked to the beach; there was a well-worn path on the upper side through the trees, but the Lancia made her feel free. It was her magic carpet, destined to whisk her to wondrous places in this beautiful land.

Across from the beach was a parking lot, a fairly good-sized one compared to the one directly in front of the Fiorito. She patted the hood of the Lancia affectionately on her way to the water.

On the beach she glanced briefly at the other bathers. Families, on holiday, had spread towels, and some were enjoying mid-day lunch.

Stripping off her skirt and top, she made herself comfortable on a beach chair and began spreading suntan lotion on her pale arms. When a beach ball skimmed past, she looked up, her quick survey causing her to do a double take.

A large-framed young woman with golden skin and long blonde hair was sunning herself—minus her bikini top. The golden girl was not the only one enjoying the sun. At least half a dozen other nubile women were also topless. One of them was a little too well endowed, and when she got up to run to the water, Caitlin stared for a moment, then looked away.

"What's the matter? Overwhelmed by the view?" The voice in her ear brought her to attention. Jake Riordan, on his haunches next to her, viewed her scowl with amusement. "You didn't know this was a topless beach, I suppose. Along this coast, most of them are."

Caitlin managed to cast him a cool look. The remorse he'd felt earlier was apparently long gone, and he was back to being his infuriating self.

He spread a blanket and stretched out near her. Black trunks defined his trim waist and long brown legs. Lean, hard and tanned all over, he matched any male physique on the beach and then some. Her heart hammering, Caitlin looked away. Best to ignore him.

She picked up a fat paperback mystery, one she'd been meaning to read for some time. Today, however, she was having trouble concentrating. The Cowboy was the problem. He sat next to her, seemingly unaware of the turmoil he was creating.

"Nice suit," he said, "although a bit prim on this beach. Perhaps tomorrow you'll emulate the sun worshippers and wear a two-piece." His inspection was unnerving. "Your-uh-attributes are every bit as enticing as theirs," he added, causing new tremors inside her.

Caitlin turned on him, stifling a retort. To say anything, was to encourage more such drivel.

Her fierce look, however, brought mock fear to his face, and he stuck up a protective hand. "Sorry," he murmured, clearly not sorry at all. She turned around, sat motionless. He was not going to give her a moment's peace, but if he thought he could rattle her...

"Actually," she said, without looking at him, 'I was just thinking about pulling down my top."

White teeth glittered in the deeply tanned face as little laugh lines formed at his eyes and mouth. "I dare you, Caitlin Harris."

Slowly she lifted her hand and began to slip a satin strap off a pale shoulder. Giving him a calm smile, she exposed a fraction of the upper swell of a creamy breast.

"Oh, dear," she murmured. "I'm still so white. Better not or I'll burn to a crisp." Flashing a nonchalant smile, she pulled up her strap and went back to her book.

She stared down at the pages unable to focus on the words. Jake's breath in her ear, his hand, sliding under her hair startled her, his touch warm on the back of her neck.

"Little fraud," he murmured. "You're far sexier covered up than they are in the buff, Cait."

She shivered. His mouth was so close, she felt as if he were dropping kisses on her lobe, his distinct male fragrance mesmerizing. This wouldn't do. She freed herself from his hold and fumbled for her sunglasses. Breathless, she reached again for her book.

"Thick book for a honeymoon, isn't it?"

Blast him! Jake had managed to remind her that she was here without a bridegroom, without anybody. Furious, she made herself focus on the mystery which she'd started on the plane.

The annoying man next to her settled back on his towel and closed his eyes. Whatever attraction the book had held was lost, but she made herself keep turning pages.

Jake sat up, uncapped a bottle of tanning lotion. Caitlin's pulses fluttered, and she turned to look at him, against her will.

"You wouldn't be kind enough to pour some of this stuff on my back, would you?"

She gazed at the muscled expanse of him, shivering at the thought of touching the bare, bronzed skin. Her "No!" came out in a semi-explosion.

"I didn't think so." Jake sighed in exaggerated fashion. "Probably be just too much excitement for you in one day."

Caitlin gasped as one firm hand, brown and lean, began massaging the lotion onto her pale, tender back.

"You're starting to burn."

She sucked in her breath sharply, warning signals going off in her head. Not that she needed them. It had been apparent from the outset, that where Jake Riordan was concerned, she was vulnerable, altogether too responsive to his brand of phony charm. She had to keep her head.

Slipping on her flats, she reached for her belongings, taking her tormentor by surprise. Loping across the beach, she was halfway to the parking lot in a matter of seconds.

The lot was nearly filled, but even from a distance she could see there was some kind of commotion. Heading for the Lancia, parked in a far corner as a protective measure, she saw a police car, siren shrieking, stop behind a large garbage truck. Both were very near where she had parked…. She blinked once, twice, half registering the loud spate of Italian exclamations. The Lancia…It couldn't be!

But, it was. Caitlin stared at her rental car in anguish and disbelief.

The once trim compact was no longer trim, a rear fender hanging, the trunk caved in on itself. Her magic carpet was crumpled, her dreams of a wondrous holiday in peril.

Chapter 2

Caitlin hung up the phone in the Fiorito's tiny office. She paused to regain her composure before turning to Signora DeLuca who had put the call through to the car rental agency for her.

"They've nothing available. With the Easter Season in full swing, every car is on the road," Caitlin told her.

The hotel owner, a small handsome woman plucked at the ruffle of her creamy, silk blouse to make it stand up and clucked sympathetically, "So now what are you going to do, Signorina?"

Caitlin shook her head in sudden despair, cursing the impulse which had made her drive to the beach lot when she could have walked the short distance through the woods.

Her reservations in the coming two weeks depended on her ability to reach the hotels by car. Public transport was out of the question, and even if she had been able to reach each destination by bus or train, she wanted her own car for exploring the surrounding countryside at each location.

There was no room at the Fiorito, Signora DeLuca having told her earlier that there wouldn't be a vacancy for two weeks.

Caitlin sighed, "I suppose I should be thankful that the police were on the spot. The driver of the garbage truck has already admitted it was his fault, so I am not liable."

"That is something to be grateful for," the older woman agreed, and patted Caitlin's arm. "Straightening out the details in such an accident can sometimes take forever. And, of course, let us be very thankful that you were not in the car. Yes?"

Caitlin smiled wanly and covered the Signora's hand with her own. Everyone had been very kind including Jake Riordan.

There was a knock on the door and the subject of Caitlin's thoughts walked in, a look of concern on his face. "Any luck?"

She shook her head. Fortunately, Jake had been right behind her at the beach, and had proved helpful in dealing with the police who had made it clear they preferred talking to a man.

Caitlin had found herself in the ridiculous position of translating for Jake who had identified himself as her companion.

Thanking Signora DeLuca for her help and the use of the phone, Caitlin started to leave, but the older woman stopped her and reached across her desk for a fax, handing it to her.

"This came for you earlier, Signorina, but in the confusion I forgot to give it to you," Signora DeLuca said.

Jake's eyebrows rose, his questioning gaze on the paper. Caitlin took it and read it, her mouth tightening as the other two looked on. Daniel, in his usual peremptory manner, was demanding to know if she was safe, demanding she come home before she came to any harm. Jamming the fax into her skirt pocket, Caitlin glanced up to see a frown on Jake's face.

She shrugged, tried to smile. "It's nothing important," she said and before he could question her made her escape from the office to the hotel sitting room.

From the wall of windows, she looked down at the shimmering azure sea dotted with small boats, sails billowing in the breeze. Oh, to be sailing right now, the wind blowing through her hair, free of any worries.

What to do? Pack up and go home? And prove to Daniel he was right? That she couldn't do without him? No way!

"But what *am* I going to do?" she muttered to herself. Visiting Europe on one's own, and for the first time, was difficult enough without surprises. The logistics of dealing with foreign currency, the exchange rate, an unfamiliar car, strange terrain, as well as the strain of having to decide everything for oneself, was not easy. But, Caitlin had accepted it readily. What she hadn't bargained for was bad luck. Earlier on she had thought of things that might go wrong, but losing her transportation was not one of them.

"I think," said Jake, "who had come quietly up behind her, "the best thing to do in a case like this is not to dwell on it. Something will come up. It always does. Try to look on the accident as another twist in your adventure."

Caitlin turned quickly to see if he were taunting her, but there was only concern in the dark blue eyes.

She flashed Jake a grateful look. He had been helpful in the parking lot, and it had been he who had suggested she call the rental agency to see if they had another car. For the moment, anyway, he had abandoned the bantering manner, which had so provoked her.

He came closer. "I've an idea," he murmured, "that a brisk shower to wash off the sand would help a lot. Then if you put on your favorite sight-seeing outfit, we could go take a look at San Margherita, have a glass of the local wine at one of the outdoor cafes, and, later, I know a very good seafood restaurant."

He was being too nice. Caitlin didn't want Jake's pity. "I would think that all the restaurants are good when it comes to fish—being right on the water," she retorted.

"Smart girl. But you wouldn't have been as intrigued if I'd said one was as good as the other, now would you?"

"What makes you think I'm interested now?'

He shrugged. "Of course, if you prefer sitting in your room all night with only a book for company…"

"No!" She'd come to see the Italian Riviera, not sit in her room moping.

"Good." His smile was dazzling. "So what do you say? Meet me back here in 30 minutes?"

She shook her head.

"All right," he conceded. "Forty-five minutes. No more." He cast an appraising look. "Girls with hair the color of ripe apricots and skin like the proverbial peaches and cream don't need much time to make themselves beautiful."

"You make me sound like a fruit salad." Caitlin's spirits lifted even as she pretended to frown. Daniel had never called her beautiful. Sensible, neat, efficient. Never beautiful.

Jake's answer was a smile. So he wouldn't see the effect he had on her, Caitlin turned toward the hall, murmuring that she'd see him shortly, very much aware that his gaze followed her to the doorway.

At the foot of the stairs she was waylaid by Tina, another of the DeLuca daughters, who had just heard about the car and wanted to offer her sympathy. She had put fresh flowers in Caitlin's room to cheer her, she told her. Tina hoped the accident would not prejudice her against Portofino.

Touched by the young girl's kindness, Caitlin stopped to chat for a moment telling her about her morning, about the beautiful lace she had seen in the vendors' stalls and the crowds which gathered this time of year in the village.

By the time she went upstairs she had already spent 10 minutes of Jake's allotted 45.

She could hear whistling in the room beyond the bath and wondered who the occupant was. A man, no doubt. Women didn't whistle like that. An aria she couldn't quite place. Verdi, maybe. Whoever it was, it didn't matter. It was unlikely she would encounter him. Besides her mind was on the evening ahead and the man she would be spending it with. Determined to enjoy herself for at least a couple of hours, she put the problem of transportation behind her.

Caitlin had just stepped out of her skirt and was unbuttoning her blouse when the whistling sounded closer and a knock on her bathroom door stopped her hand.

"Yes?" she called. No answer. The knock was repeated.

"What is it?" she called again. Still no answer. Someone who didn't speak English? Dragging her skirt back on over her swimsuit and buttoning her shirt, she cautiously opened the door.

"What you're not undressed yet? How do you expect to be on time? I like my dates to be punctual." Jake pretended to glower.

Her mouth hung open. "What are you doing in my bathroom!"

"It's my bathroom, too."

"You're in the next…?" She broke off weakly.

He nodded, pretending to leer. "You can have the first shower if you promise not to leave your stockings and unmentionables dripping on the shower rod."

"I never do!"

"I wouldn't mind that much." Jake grinned. "If they're as fancy as the nightgown you had on this morning, it'd be an edifying…"

Caitlin shut the door in his face. She turned her back only to hear him reopen it a crack. "Only 30 minutes left…"

She shut the door again, this time bolting it from her side. Grabbing a robe, she shed her clothes, then opened the bathroom door to make sure Jake was not lurking there. It was empty, and going in, she bolted the connecting door to his room. She wouldn't put it past him to come in and check on her progress.

The bathroom, like the rest of the hotel, was quaintly old-fashioned, but efficient enough if you didn't mind holding a shower hose in one hand and lathering your hair with the other.

Caitlin made short work of her ablutions and winding a towel about her damp hair, dried herself off and donned the robe.

Without turning, she called over her shoulder, hoping Jake would hear. "It's all yours…" And going through to her bedroom she once again bolted the door behind her and started going through her all too ordinary outfits. In shopping for a trousseau, she had splurged only on nightwear, thinking to replenish her day clothes from Italian shops. How shortsighted of her. She frowned going through her choices again.

It was only a moment before her hall door was resounding with loud blows. Now what? Caitlin put down a cotton top she was holding, went to the door and found an indignant Jake, clad only in a towel he'd wrapped around his waist

"It would help you know," he blustered, " if you would remember to unlock my door to the bathroom before you leave."

The look on Jake's face was comical and she started to laugh, which had a dangerous effect on him. "I'll do it right now." She moved to close the door on him, but a large hand prevented her.

"Let me go through your room. It's faster. Tina is coming down the hall with a load of linens, and I'm sure her mother would not appreciate her running into me dressed as I am."

He pushed past her, ignoring her protests, and stood hands on hips, scowling at the sight of the already-bolted door to the bathroom

"My God, you must have been raised in a convent, Cait, my love," he muttered, "not every man is out to ravish you." And going into the bathroom, he slammed the door behind him.

Caitlin made a face, debating for only a second before again securing the door. The "snick" of the bolt sliding home brought a humorless, "Ha!" from the other side.

Donning underwear, Caitlin ran her hands through her hair. The warmth of the day and the gentle breeze filling the room was drying it quickly. Now to get dressed.

Again, nothing pleased her. Everything looked too...too serviceable.

Settling on a green and white striped cotton dress she pulled it over her head and made a face at the sight in the wavy mirror.

Her hair. No way was she going to bunch it into a barrette. Finding some hairpins in her cosmetic case, she began piling it on top of her head, picking out little tendrils to fall about her ears.

Earrings. The white enamel. No, the gold hoops. They'd lend an exotic air, she hoped. Shoes were no problem. She was proud of her slim ankles and the high-heeled sandals did nice things for her long legs.

Caitlin touched perfume to her throat and wrists and reminded herself to choose another fragrance when she had a chance. This had been a gift from Daniel and was not subtle enough to suit her.

When Jake knocked on the hall door this time, she was ready for him. Caitlin surveyed the white slacks, pale blue shirt and navy jacket. His dark hair was still damp, making it curl just above his collar. He wore after-shave she didn't recognize.

"We're going to clash," she told him and Jake look puzzled, explained, "Our perfume. Mine's floral and yours is spicy."

Jake shook his head in amusement. "Men don't wear perfume. Well, some do," he allowed, "but they give it a macho handle."

Caitlin reached for a white, gauzy wrap. "What do you call yours?"

"You've heard of *Savage*?

"Umm."

"Brute?"

"Umm."

He bared his teeth. "Mine is *Cannibal*."

Caitlin burst out laughing, her heart light.

"It was his turn to assess her. "You look very...charming."

Caitlin flushed, feeling drab as he gave her the once over.

"Well, you will when we correct one little thing." Lean brown fingers went to her bodice and before she had time to do more than suck in her breath, he had undone the top button. His warm touch scorched her skin.

She managed to thrust his fingers away as he commented, "That's enough for now, anyway. After you've had a glass or two of

Pinot San Margherita, you may feel the need to undo some more buttons yourself."

And with that, Jake ushered her into the hall, held out his hand for her key, locked the door, and then returned it to her.

The vintage Mercedes, beautifully restored, had its top down. "What is your Italian friend doing with a German car?" Caitlin asked, admiring the leather interior.

"Inherited it, I think. From an uncle who traveled a lot. " They drove slowly along the winding sea road, past the bathing beach and the parking lot where her car had been hit. Caitlin blocked out the anxiety that threatened to upend her.

She closed her eyes in hopes of imprinting the magnificent setting permanently on her brain. Jake took the curves slowly, and she let the gentle breeze from the sea wash over her. To her surprise a sense of well being had sprung from some inner place when she knew she should be worrying about the hotel reservations and the fax from Daniel. She had transferred his message from her skirt pocket to her handbag, and she knew she'd have to deal with it at some point.

But she wasn't going to ruin this outing. For now at least she would do what Jake had demanded: Put everything out of her mind except the fact that she was in one of the most beautiful, unspoiled spots in the entire world.

Jake parked the convertible in a municipal lot, and they began their stroll on the far side of the resort. It was late afternoon, and traffic was heavy in the town of San Margherita so they made for the small seaside park.

Located across from a block of shops and restaurants, it was filled with trees and exotic flowers and boasted an occasional wooden bench.

Jake paused at one of the benches, and Caitlin sank down gracefully taking in the scent of flowers, the blue of sky and sea and the fishing boats in the distance.

She sighed with pleasure, and Jake grinned down at her. Nudging her over, he sat down and slid an arm behind her. "Enjoying yourself?"

Caitlin nodded, not trusting herself to speak. Her senses were awash with the glittering sea, the colorful architecture, and the heady scent of flowers. She'd never felt more alive, particularly with this man so close to her.

Jake pointed to a large ship on the horizon. "You stick with old Jake, and we'll make you forget your troubles which, if you are honest with yourself, are very small ones. Right?"

Caitlin nodded again, alarmed at the happiness that welled within. The sea air, scented with oleander, was making her tipsy. That had to be it.

They sat in companionable silence a while longer, then Jake's hand under her elbow brought Caitlin to her feet. "Let's go explore the town, find a place to try some local wine and we'll get to know one another." He gave her a wry smile, "Caitlin Harris, are you aware that all we've done since we met is spar?"

She returned the smile and let him pilot her across the park to the shops where they peered into windows, discreetly inspected the natives and sampled some wares.

At an *alimentari,* a huge pie in the window of the Italian-style deli caught Jake's attention. "Will you look at that! It has to be two feet across."

They entered the shop and Jake demanded Caitlin ask the proprietor, a brawny fellow with mustache and shirtsleeves rolled to the elbow, what it was.

"Come se chiama questa?" she said obediently, pointing to the pie.

"Torta Pasqualina," came the reply followed by a lengthy explanation.

"It's called Easter Pie," she translated for Jake. "They make it here, a specialty of the region, only during the holiday. It has artichoke hearts, ricotta cheese and hard-boiled eggs among other things. Do you want to try it?"

"Do camels have humps? Is the Pope Catholic? Of course, I want to try it. We both do." He squeezed her arm, his breath fragrant on her cheek.

The man behind the counter cut a generous slice and transferred it to a piece of white butcher paper, then weighed it. Caitlin could feel Jake just behind her, not quite touching. No mere slip of a woman, her sandals gave her added inches. Still, Jake towered over her.

Accepting the proffered pie, Caitlin waited until Jake fished out the correct coins and they made their way to the wooden booths at the back of the store.

Jake squeezed in next to her instead of sitting across from her, explaining that they should leave room in case other customers should come in.

Caitlin didn't take the trouble of pointing out that there were two other booths unoccupied, and no one was likely to sit in the same booth with them.

She was growing accustomed to having Jake next to her. Some portion of her mind told her to be wary. But another superior level of her brain was contradictive, pointing out that in this lovely, fecund part of the world all creatures should be paired off. And, why should she be alone because her fiancé—her ex-fiancé—had preferred business to her.

The *torta* was delicious, though Caitlin thought it probably would be even better warm. The glazed crust was flaky, the inside a wondrous medley of texture and flavor. She smiled at Jake who was wolfing down his portion.

"You didn't have any lunch?"

He swallowed before speaking. " Very little. Antipasto, spaghetti pescadore, half a loaf of bread and a liter of wine. Dinner in Italy doesn't start until after eight. I had to be fortified."

Caitlin stared in amazement, her gaze going to his trim waist. "You can't eat like that at home?"

"Nope. Only when I'm at our Providence inn.

"The Italian chef and his olive oil?"

He nodded. "Tell me again what was in the pie. I'll make a note of it so I can tell Raffaele."

She told him as they strolled about, Caitlin taking in a hair salon and several clothing shops

.   At a small outdoor café, Jake called a halt and they relaxed with a carafe of draft wine. Caitlin was amused to see that the waiter poured it into small tumblers rather than wineglasses.

Across the small table, Jake raised his eyebrows as she pushed her empty glass toward him for a refill.

"We've a lot of evening ahead of us. How about if I mix the wine with the *aqua minerale*? He reached for the bottle of water he had asked the waiter to bring.

When she nodded, he poured half and half in her glass. Caitlin pronounced it "fine" then added, "though I think I prefer the wine by itself best."

"Spoken like a true wino," Jake teased, but she noticed he didn't dilute his own drink.

The wine had relaxed her. She hadn't thought of the damaged car the whole time she'd been with Jake. Tonight might be all she had of this kind of adventure, and she wasn't going to spoil it." Tomorrow was soon enough to worry about solutions.

Jake was smiling at her. A penny for your thoughts?"

"Oh, just how lovely it is here. It's almost too much to take in. And the people are so warm and kind." She went on telling him how supportive Signora DeLuca and her daughters had been.

"Then you're not lonely here by yourself."

"No, I've never been abroad before, but I've seen a lot of America. I'm known as the traveler in the family. I did a lot with friends during college breaks."

"Is that right?" Jake seemed amused. She drank in the sight of him across from her. Thick, springy brown hair, lean, interesting face.

"Tell me more about Caitlin Harris. A very intriguing subject."

"Not really." She was uncomfortable with his scrutiny.

"But of course you are. How many other women do you know who would defy convention and go off on a honeymoon trip by themselves?" He was laughing, but not at her, and she decided not to take offense.

"Lots of women travel by themselves these days. All over the world."

"Not on wedding trips minus the bridegroom."

She didn't want to talk about Daniel. Didn't want to think about him. She changed the subject abruptly, mentioning the lace they had seen in one of the windows, how she was smitten with old things, especially handmade, about the antique quilt collection she was amassing, how lucky she'd been to find the Italian-born Antonietta to help her in her shop.

She stopped abruptly. She was talking too much, but Jake hadn't seemed to notice. His eyes crinkling at the corner, one brown finger gently moving back and forth across her wrist, he urged her on, wanting to know more about Caitlin Harris. Her natural reserve lessened by the wine, she told him.

Her brother Kenny lived in southern California, and her younger sister Liz was married to Joe, her high school sweetheart. Caitlin loved playing the doting aunt to baby Jessica. They lived only a few blocks from the family home, which now seemed too big, even though Gran had moved in after Grandpa had died.

"An extended family. I thought they went out with the nuclear age?"

Jake seemed really interested, not just being polite and soon she was telling him about Gran's auto accident and how when her grandmother had been released from the hospital, Caitlin had given up her own small apartment to come home and help her mother nurse her. Caitlin hadn't really minded giving up her own place, not since she believed she was going to be married soon anyway...

Jake frowned, then drained his glass. "Tell me about your fiancé. What did you say his name is? Daniel?"

"Daniel Sloane. Old family, old money." She clipped the words.

"How did you meet?"

She kept the recitation to the barest of facts. She'd needed to insure her small workshop where she sometimes kept clients' priceless possessions. She'd gone to his office to meet with another agent about a policy. When she arrived the agent had had an emergency at home and Daniel, himself, had walked past as the secretary was informing her of the need to make a new appointment. He had been on his way out, but stopped and invited her into his office and taken care of it himself. They began dating and within months were engaged.

"Whirlwind courtship, hmm? Jake twirled his empty tumbler. "What does your family think of him?"

She chose her words with care. As the wine further loosened her tongue, she told of the clashes between Daniel and her beloved grandmother. How Daniel didn't approve of Gran's sometimes salty comments she'd picked up from her sailor husband. Caitlin repeated her grandmother's blunt, colorful words upon learning of Daniel's "working honeymoon" plan causing Jake to suppress a grin.

If Jake thought Daniel's reserving an extra room at each hotel strange behavior for a bridegroom, he refrained from commenting, asking instead, "And Daniel's opinion of the rest of your family?"

Caitlin hesitated, then shrugged. "Daniel thinks us all a little common, I suspect. He thinks Gran's brand of humor not befitting an older woman. It also bothers him to see her drink an occasional glass of beer."

Jake's mouth curved. "Old Daniel's something of a prude?"

Caitlin smiled. "Well, Gran does bait him sometimes. She's a bit of an imp. You'll love her, Jake. Everybody does. Everybody, but Daniel..." She broke off as she realized what she had said. As if she were going to take Jake home to meet the family...

Jake didn't seem to notice her slip. "Daniel. So you met him at his office and that was that... Apparently he knew quality when he saw it." Before Caitlin had time to dwell on that comment, he burst her bubble. "The fax Signora DeLuca gave you. It was from him, wasn't it?"

Jake's voice suddenly had an edge to it. "You're going to fax him back, aren't you?" It was a statement, not a question. "Only fair to let him know you're safe and sound."

"Maybe. Or maybe not." There was a fax machine at Caitlin's shop. She'd promised to contact Antonietta regularly who would then call Caitlin's family to assure them she was fine traveling alone. Daniel knew he could call Caitlin's assistant for an update. Defiant in the face of challenge, she shifted in her chair aware that Jake was frowning. The conversation was becoming very one-sided.

"How about you?" she asked in an attempt to shift the focus away from herself and Daniel. "I've told you all about me, and I know nothing about Jake Riordan other than that you own some inns and take silly dares." Out of habit she glanced down at his feet. But, this time he'd left the boots behind.

His frown changed to a smile as he followed her glance. "The Stetson's in the car trunk. I can go get it and put it on if you like. And, it's not a silly dare. It's a bet. I stand to collect a bundle if I can prove I've worn them."

"How much of a bundle?"

"Fifty big ones."

Caitlin shot him a look. Fifty dollars to Jake was pin money, she suspected.

He laughed, again reading her mind. "It's the principle of the thing."

"Who dubbed you Jake?"

His amusement deepened, and she heard a rumble deep in his broad chest. "My mother. Before I was born, she kept telling Dad, 'Jake's really kicking up a storm today, or Jake didn't cotton to the chili peppers I ate last night.'"

Caitlin grinned. "And it stuck?"

"Like jam."

"You look like a Jake," Caitlin murmured, the wine now having produced a rosy haze that made the view even more beautiful. Come to think of it, Jake was beautiful, too, but she wouldn't make the mistake of telling him that. At least she hoped not. In her current state, no telling what might come out of her mouth.

Jake's hand came to cover hers where it rested on her glass. "Come on, sweet Cait, time for us to walk around a bit and get some fresh sea air and then we'll choose a restaurant." And taking her arm, he guided her to her feet.

The breeze from the harbor did the trick. The wine-induced cobwebs began to disperse. They strolled through the streets, taking side avenues to peek in designer boutiques, hole-in-the-wall bookshops and miniature art galleries. Was there nothing about this place that was not wonderful?

"Enchanting!" Caitlin murmured.

"Agreed," Jake said, looking down at her and smiling. For a moment she had the feeling he was talking about her, but these things didn't happen in so short a time.

The restaurant they settled on much later was rustic in character. Earlier in their walking about they had seen fishermen trucking in the day's catch straight from their boats. "Can't get much fresher," Caitlin said.

Bare wooden floors, unadorned tables, oil lamps hanging from the rafters and old fishing nets stretched across the walls comprised the decorations.

They started with *contorni;* a medley of cold vegetables sautéed lightly in olive oil, and followed the initial course with savory rice dotted with tiny clams in the shell. Washed down with the local wine, of course.

"It's a sight to see how they bring the draft wine in," Jake said. "A truck pulls up out front with a large hose that is connected to barrels in the cellar. Just like fuel trucks at home."

"But much better tasting," said Caitlin taking another sip. She couldn't remember when she had enjoyed herself as much. Normal inhibitions seemed to dissolve in this magical place.

As they lingered over espresso, Jake turned the subject again to the fax she had received earlier in the day.

"You are going to answer it, yes?"

Jake was beginning to sound like a broken record. She gave him a look. "Why are you so concerned?"

The question seemed to take him aback, but he recovered quickly. "If it were my fiancée, I would be very much concerned about her safety."

"He's not...." She broke off. Caitlin was determined to put Daniel behind her, but she didn't think she wanted Jake to know that.

A man of Jake's looks and charm probably had a lot of girls chasing after him. Caitlin wasn't eager to be included in that category. If Jake thought she was going back to Daniel, he wouldn't feel threatened by her presence. And after the last few years with Daniel, she needed some time alone, to think about men, her life and her future.

Smoothly, she turned the tables. "Enough about my life. What about you?"

"What about me?" Jake's eyes were suddenly guarded even though he was smiling. He rolled the small glass between his palms. His eyes were very blue and for a moment, Caitlin felt as if she could swim in their depths.

She let her gaze travel once more over his lean profile. "I guess you to be this side of 35 and still single." There she'd said it.

"Correct on both counts."

She breathed deeply, hoping he wouldn't see the effect his words had on her. She hadn't thought him attached, but one could never tell.

"You must have had many girls or" …something seemed to catch in her throat, "one special one."

"Aren't all girls special?"

"Don't be obtuse."

"What do you mean by special?" he said at last.

"Someone you care a lot about."

Again, there was a long pause. "You could say so."

Emotion shot through Caitlin, taking her by surprise. She paused for a moment before asking, "What's she like?"

Jake's eyes softened. "Umm, small, petite, black curly hair, blue eyes. Just a little older than you."

The feelings of a moment before accelerated, leaving a strange feeling in her chest. "Have you a picture of her?"

For a moment, she thought he hadn't heard her, then his hand went to his pocket. He paused again before retrieving a slim wallet from which he withdrew a snapshot. There were two women in the photo, one an attractive older woman with Jake's smile. She and the small brunette had their arms about each other's waists.

Caitlin focused on the younger woman. Not pretty in a conventional way, but there was definitely something about her—a fey kind of beauty.

She inhaled. "What's her name?"

He took back the photo and smiled at the figures. "The older woman is my mother. She's Barbara, Bibi for short. Jenny lives next door, but she's at our house as much as her own. She has only her father, and Bibi has been surrogate mother to her since Jenny was a little girl. Bibi is very eager to get her into the family."

Caitlin glanced again at the photo. The evening's magic had just evaporated, and the room which had seemed so open before now threatened to suffocate her.

"So when's the big day?" To cover her feelings, she began playing with the small lantern in the center of the table.

"The wedding you mean? Oh, nothing's been settled yet. More of an agreement at this point."

"Oh," Caitlin's voice was barely audible to her own ears.

"Our families are close. Dad, my brother Harry and Jenny's father go fishing together, that sort of thing. They're included in all our holiday celebrations, in fact in most of our family life. Not a bad basis for a marriage, I suppose."

Wrong, wrong, Caitlin wanted to shout. There should be love and commitment with at least a dash of chemistry thrown in, qualities which she now realized had been in short supply in her and Daniel's relationship.

Jake didn't seem too worked up talking about Jenny either. But, maybe that's the way they did things in his circle. Compatibility was the important thing. Love, if it came at all, came after the wedding. Just as in arranged marriages of old.

Maybe such things weren't important to Jake. He was certainly casual about it all. Almost as if he'd never given it a thought beyond the here and now. Typical male.

Suddenly all the fun had gone out of the evening. Her head was aching and one of her earrings had begun to pinch. She took off the gold hoop and stuck it on her finger, then gently massaged the tender lobe.

When she looked up, Jake's gaze was on her hand. With trepidation she realized she'd stuck it on her ring finger, his expression easy to interpret. He thought Caitlin was missing Daniel, that she regretted giving back her engagement ring. Good. Let him think it. It would keep Jake from thinking she was mourning the man across from her, mourning the fact that he had Jenny back home waiting to marry him. As if she cared. She had enough of men and their self-absorbed ways.

Caitlin's headache was worse. The troubles she had temporarily put aside were coming back with a vengeance.

The thought of the crumpled car, no longer hers to use, tore at her. She felt like crying. The evening had become shambles.

"I think I should be getting back," she said faintly. She was tired, very tired. She'd had too much wine, too much moonlight, and too much Riviera magic.

Caitlin stood, wobbling a little on her high heels, and Jake immediately called for their check. Quickly settling their account, he put one hand under her elbow, and guided her out of the restaurant, down the street to the car.

By the light of the moon, Caitlin could see the orange trees lining the main San Margherita thoroughfare. Bright orangish green globes hung heavy from the branches. Earlier in the day she had thought how beautiful they were. It had not been until they were directly underneath the trees that Jake had reached up and plucked a couple and discovered they had gone bad, victims of municipal neglect. That's how her evening had turned out. Spoiled. An optical illusion.

Jake opened the car door and put her inside. It took them only minutes to travel the winding sea road, a three-quarter moon casting its glow.

Very soon they were in the Fiorito's miniature parking lot. Hurrying up the steps into the lobby, Caitlin said goodnight to Jake without looking around. She made for the stairs, still not conscious whether or not he was behind her. Happily no one was around.

In the bathroom she washed her face and brushed her teeth, making sure she didn't catch her reflection in the mirror above. She didn't want to see the sad image she knew would be looking back at her.

Once in bed, she vowed not to think of anything. She would just go to sleep. One tear slid down her cheek. Damn. It was the wine. It always left her feeling morose when she drank more than a glass.

She bit back the tears, hiccupped in the process and started giggling. She hiccupped again. The wine and the anchovies that had topped the salad were battling.

She made it to the bathroom just in time. Caitlin didn't hear the other door open, knew only of Jake's presence as he pressed a wet washcloth in her hand. She wiped her face, mortified that he was seeing her like this.

"Better?" he asked quietly.

She didn't trust herself to speak, and nodded yes.

"Good. Let's get you back to bed."

He led the way into her room, the light shining from his, illuminating it dimly. He turned on the lamp beside her bed and watched as she came toward him in the apricot silk gown. Caitlin was too undone to worry about affording him another glimpse of her in the gossamer nightdress. Besides, what did anything matter now? He pulled back the covers and waited until she was settled before turning off the lamp. Caitlin turned her back to him and waited for him to leave. She hoped she'd never have to see him again.

Instead, she felt the mattress depress as he sat down. One large hand smoothed her hair. "Are you sure you're all right?"

"Yes, thank you." Why didn't he go?

He didn't. Rather he rearranged his large frame to make himself comfortable. She was tired, extremely so. What was he doing just sitting there?

Caitlin half dozed off, too weary to worry about the proprieties, when she felt his hand on her hair, again. Then, it moved. This time his hand settled lower, making light, comforting circles on the small of her back.

Even in her daze, she knew it was a comforting gesture, the way Liz soothed a colicky Jessica.

Caitlin settled deeper into the bed. In a moment she would rouse and tell Jake Riordan, Jenny's intended, that he was not to take such liberties.

In the distance, a ship's whistle resounded over the water and a breeze from the sea gently played with the gauzy curtains at the open French doors. The comforting movement of Jake's hand on her back continued. A sigh for what might have been escaped her and Caitlin sank into a deep sleep.

Chapter 3

Caitlin's descent to the lobby the next morning was anything but lighthearted. It was amazing how physically well she felt after her embarrassing lapse of the night before. Her mental state was another matter. She had made a fool of herself in front of Jake Riordan. Aided by the magic of the evening and the wine, she'd also convinced herself she felt something for him. Talk about rebounding! Now the last thing she wanted to do was sit across from him at breakfast.

In hopes of avoiding Jake, she bypassed the breakfast room and sought out Signora DeLuca in her office. The hotel owner was about to leave for San Margherita to do some banking, and Caitlin begged a ride from her. Not only did she get a gracious, "of course," but was shepherded through the office's rear exit to the private garage.

"You dined with Signore Riordan last evening?" the older woman asked as she put the car, an ancient, but smooth-running model, into gear.

Caitlin nodded, and Signora DeLuca smiled in satisfaction. "He is a gentleman. We have mutual friends, the Cimino family in Rome, who are also in the hotel business."

She shot Caitlin a searching glance as she took the curves of the sea road at slow speed. "It is good you have such an escort. You can trust him."

She paused for a moment as if debating with herself, then her mouth set in a thin line, revealed, "My daughter Tina has told me a male guest has been asking about you. He wanted to know if you were traveling alone and what room you were in."

The woman's aquiline nose seemed to grow sharper as she grated, " I had a stern talk with Tina. Thank goodness she knew enough not to reveal your room location. The guest checked out this morning, but there are others who could do you harm…"

Glancing sideways at Caitlin, and seeing her stare straight ahead, Signora DeLuca sighed. "Perhaps I am being too negative, Signorina Harris, but please be careful in your travels. You still have not resolved the problem of transportation? The trains, perhaps?

Caitlin shook her head to both questions and the older woman surprised her by offering her one of the cramped rooms on the top floor that the family used during the height of the tourist season.

She apologized for having nothing better available. "It is, however, clean and well-ventilated and the bed is quite comfortable."

"You are very kind, Signora, and I appreciate your offer more than I can say, but I have had my heart set on this trip for so long I have to find a way to carry it out, "Caitlin murmured.

"You will," came the assurance. "Perhaps Signore Riordan will have an idea. He is very concerned. He was already in to see me this morning regarding your lack of a car.

The mention of Jake set Caitlin scrambling to find another subject. Admiring the signora's printed silk scarf worn loosely under her suit jacket, Caitlin hit upon Italian fashion.

Italians, even those with modest means, were devoted to looking their best at all times, she had discovered. Men and women, alike, might skimp on certain necessities in order to afford clothing and accessories of good quality. B*ella figura* was a matter of presenting oneself to advantage in every way possible, a concept Caitlin was taking new interest in.

Being here amid all these style-conscious people had made her aware of her own shortcomings. Should she run into Jake again, an unlikely possibility, she wanted him to see her at her best as an antidote to last night's humiliating ending. In any case, she was determined to liven up her own wardrobe. It occurred to her she had a lot of living to do to make up for the Daniel years when he had quashed any changes other than those he initiated.

Signora DeLuca was more than happy to discuss fashion. By the end of the short trip, Caitlin had been given several tips as to which shops offered the best selections, which had inflated prices and where the best Italian leather shoes and bags could be found.

Dropping her off near the seaside park, Signora DeLuca wished her a pleasant day and urged Caitlin to seek her out if she could be of any further assistance, reminding her of the Fiorito's phone number.

Caitlin's first stop was at an outdoor café where she enjoyed the typical Italian breakfast of coffee and a hard roll. An unobstructed view of the sparkling sea, billowing sails and cloudless sky were not wasted on her.

Did the water seem less blue this morning? The Riviera resort with its palms and pastel architecture less delightful? No, even if she was alone, without Daniel *or* Jake, the scene swamped her senses.

Jake's revelation the night before that he and the girl next door had an understanding had been something of a shock. Although why it should have been was not clear to Caitlin. It would have been strange if someone of Jake's charm, good looks and affability was unattached.

Thoughts of attachments reminded her of the telegram now lying folded in a tiny square in the bottom of her purse. She fished it out, smoothing it, reading again Daniel's terse message. How like him to order her home! She had been very much aware of his dogmatic streak, aware that he lorded it over her, but because she had loved him, she had overlooked it.

Had loved him. She repeated the words aloud, the unconscious choice of tense, disturbing. Had she ever loved Daniel, or had it been a matter of initial awe and admiration dissolving into habit?

Just being with someone else for a few hours had made Caitlin realize how flimsy her feelings for Daniel had been. How selfish and inconsiderate he was under the suave exterior. Oh, he'd been generous with gifts, but she'd had the feeling each had been presented with the underlying purpose of making her more worthy of his attention.

Sighing, she thrust the fax back into her bag and pulled out the throwaway camera she had purchased the day before.

Walking the short distance to the park, she took pictures of the fishing boats, the exotic flowers and the buildings that fronted on the park. A boy and girl, both under 10, were admiring a sporty red Ferrari parked near the pier.

As she approached, they spotted the camera and begged her to take their picture next to the car and, smiling, she waited until they assumed proprietary poses and snapped away.

"It's not an instant" she explained in Italian, but it was of no importance.

"Grazie." They were delighted to simply have been captured on film in the proximity of the expensive car.

Caitlin crossed back to the row of shops and began peering in the windows. The casual resort clothes, their bright hues and relaxed, but fashionable, styles delighted her.

Making mental notes as she walked along, she came across a hairdressing salon just as a young man with curly black hair and tight jeans unlocked the front door.

Caitlin's hands went to her pulled-back hair. Daniel had always insisted she keep it long, not because he found it sexy, but because he abhorred the short, sleek styles so many women in his company effected.

"Scusi," she began and within minutes was seated inside the shop with Gino's skilled fingers turning her head this way and that to determine what cut would best show off the signorina's pretty face.

"*Bella, bella,*" he said as she looked in the mirror and again after she paid the rather hefty price and was walking out of the shop. But catching sight of her new style she decided it was worth every bit. She did, indeed, feel beautiful after the half-hour of harmless flirting and expert cutting.

Gino had cut several inches from her hair and her head felt light and airy. Encouraged by her reflection in the shop window, Caitlin made straight for a dress shop which 30 minutes before she had dismissed as being too expensive.

If some solution didn't present itself, she could soon be headed home. Better to spend the money and have something to take back to remind her that she had had at least a taste of the continent.

The shop clerk, a woman near Caitlin's age, gave her the same appraising look Gino had. In a moment she had gathered an armful of outfits for Caitlin's inspection.

Colorful pants, skirts and tops started to pile up until Caitlin called a halt. At this rate she'd have to cash in her return ticket. But the shop's periwinkle bags with the silver logo that filled her arms on the way out gave her a much-needed lift.

Caitlin threaded her way through the vacation crowds, which were now filling the streets. She felt like one of them, free and independent. Suddenly she caught sight of a tow truck pulling a small car, and the euphoria of the past hour faded.

A decision had to be made. She had only one more night at the Fiorito. Kind as Signora DeLuca had been about offering her one of the family rooms, Caitlin had come to see Italy, not to stay stranded in one spot, even if that spot was the gorgeous Ligurian coast.

She moved pensively down the sidewalk, retracing the route Jake and she had taken the day before. Her spirits dimmed even more as she remembered his banter and sense of adventure. If only...

Head down, she was not aware of the man next to her until he bumped into her. It seemed almost deliberate, and she was sure of it a moment later when he kept his hand on her arm as he pretended concern for her well being. He spoke English but there was an accent and Caitlin guessed French or possibly German. She brushed him off hastily, not liking the touch of his fingers nor the light in the dark, too bright eyes.

Signora DeLuca was right. She had to be more careful. She moved away quickly. A firm grasp on her elbow just after she had increased her speed, caught her by surprise and she turned, fire in her eyes.

Anger melted as she saw whose grasp she was in, and relieved, she let Jake pull her close to him.

"Are you all right?" he demanded without letting her go. " I was across the street and saw it all. That cretin bumped into you deliberately. I feel like going after him," he muttered.

"It's all right," Caitlin murmured, surprised by his presence. "Nothing happened," she added and moved out of his arms only to be buoyed when he placed his hand on the small of her back and guided her toward the Mercedes parked a short distance away.

"Where have you been all morning? I've been searching the town for you. Marisa said you got a ride with her mother..." Jake stopped abruptly and took in the new hairdo, his gaze softening.

"Very nice...lets me see more of your face...what's in the packages?"

He focused on the shop's logo, stylized silver letters on the periwinkle bags. "Don't tell me you are going to go ultra chic on me?"

"And if I do?" She clutched the bundles to her as if he were going to snatch them from her.

Jake chuckled. "Nothing. Except why mess around with a near perfect product?"

A suffocating warmth stole over Caitlin, her heart lurching foolishly. He mustn't say things like that. She mustn't take him seriously, but the look in his eyes was anything but bogus. Jake. Jake. Why hadn't she met him before? Before he promised himself to the girl next door? To Jenny, the girl that his mother adored.

Caitlin let Jake hand her into the car and soon they were headed out of town toward the village of Portofino. Her clamoring senses kept her from asking what he had in mind, but as before Jake read her thoughts.

"It's lunch time." He consulted his watch. "Well, a little early according to Italian custom, but I thought we'd beat the crowds. I found a little place yesterday when you refused to go shopping with me. The pasta was *magnifico*. Or you can have something lighter if you prefer…" He glanced at her, his warm questioning look bringing a flush to Caitlin's face?

"Anything will do," she said in a quiet voice hoping he would not catch the note of elation in it.

She was silent as they drove the winding road along the sea, passing the Fiorito on their way. Tina, dark blue apron over her dress, was sweeping down the stone steps and catching sight of them, waved. Caitlin, on a cloud of happiness, waved back, reflecting that the Fiorito was well named. Small, but a jewel in a garden paradise.

Granted, it was a paradise with problems. But she was with Jake, and she was not about to spoil the little time she had left with him by dwelling on them.

In the small, white-walled restaurant with modern curving banquettes and round tables, Jake seated her and then pushed in next to her. A dim, cool haven in the brilliant sunshine, the restaurant was nearly empty. As Jake had said the midday meal for Italians had not yet begun.

Taking her at her word, he ordered lunch, the waiter having assured him he was fluent in four languages. Here in Europe with people from one country moving easily across borders, the French, the Germans, the Belgians and Spaniards found as much reason to come to this beautiful spot as Americans did. She imagined it didn't take long for a waiter to pick up the various tongues.

Caitlin sipped slowly from her glass, which held, at her request, a mixture of aqua minerale and wine.

Jake watched her, smiling. She thought he started to say something but then stopped. Once more it happened. Then he spoke. "I've a suggestion for you," he said without preamble. "I don't know why it didn't occur to me before. About your trip, I mean."

"What about it?" Caitlin felt herself drowning in the depths of the sea-blue eyes. I think I've exhausted the possibilities."

"No, you haven't," he interrupted. He drank sparingly, watching her over the rim of his glass. "I want you to hear what I have to say, all of it, before you answer. Deal?"

"Deal," she said slowly, her curiosity aroused.

"First things first," Jake said. "Did you answer the fax from your fiancé?"

Caitlin shook her head.

Jake frowned. "The issue here is to put his mind at rest. That is, if you plan on staying in Europe..."

"I'm staying," said Caitlin, announcing with conviction that which she had been debating a very short while before.

"Good. Make sure you get back to him then. Fax or call him. It's the considerate thing to do. Might even save you some problems later on."

Caitlin was silent. She'd promised her shop assistant she would fax her every so often with the information to be forwarded on to her parents. Far easier than phoning. especially with the different time zones. Maybe she'd put Daniel's mind at ease. Maybe she wouldn't. The way he'd treated her didn't call for any special favors.

"So what's your idea?" she asked, her relief tangible at having made the decision to continue her trip.

He paused, said slowly, "Last night you told me how Daniel reserved a connecting extra room at each hotel for business purposes." She nodded. "And that you planned at each stop to have the reservation changed back to one room, if possible, just as you did at the Fiorito."

She nodded again. That had been her intention, still was, provided she could get to her destinations. If the Easter season was as busy as the crowds in Portofino and San Margherita indicated, the hotels should be happy to get back an extra room.

"This trip really means a lot to you, doesn't it? "

"Yes." Who knew when she'd get another chance to see this lovely part of the world?

Jake reached over, put one large tanned hand on top of hers. Warmth surged through her. She evaded the intense look in his eyes and wondered what it would be like to wake next to this man for the next 50 plus years. She blushed at her own thoughts and hoped that Jake who had shown a particular talent for knowing what she was thinking, hadn't tuned in this time.

But Jake was focused elsewhere. He restated her situation. "You have reserved an extra room at each location but no way of getting there. Correct?"

"No practical way. Trains, buses possibly. But, I'd have to spend all my time traveling, making connections, worrying about delays."

Jake's hand lifted, his fingers brushing back and forth over her knuckles reminding her how he had comforted her the night before after she became sick. Her cheeks grew warmer.

"Now, I, on the other hand," he continued, "have no reservations, but do have a very fast, efficient, and comfortable car at my disposal for the next couple of weeks."

Caitlin stared at him, suddenly getting his drift but not quite daring to draw the conclusion she was obviously meant to. "What are you saying?"

Jake was matter of fact. "We team up. Your rooms, my car."

"What?" Hearing it stated so matter-of-factly started her pulses pounding.

"It's very simple. We take my car—Paolo's car—and travel about just as you planned. You see your sights. I get to check out some small inns, talk to the owners. We share your spacious accommodations."

Her voice was not quite steady. "Together?"

Jake laughed, the husky tones vibrating up and down her spine. "Together, but apart."

"You want us to travel together, check in together…"

"Good girl," he praised as if she had just mastered the theory of relativity.

She flushed at the gentle sarcasm. "But…"

"But what? I've got it all figured out. Hotel managements are used to this kind of arrangement. Business people do it all the time. There's nothing even remotely scandalous about an unattached man and woman sharing a suite or connecting rooms..."

Caitlin flashed him a look. "Maybe not to you." She thought of her unsophisticated parents, the fact that she and Daniel had been engaged until very recently.

Granted she was an adult, in full possession of her faculties, and she had come thousands of miles to fulfill a dream. But to travel around the country, occupy adjoining rooms with a man she had met 24 hours before?

This time Jake was tuned in. "I think that after last night, Cait, we're hardly strangers."

Her face flamed as she vividly recalled being sick in the bathroom, Jake's putting her to bed, his large hand gently smoothing her back, soothing her to sleep.

"If I had wanted to take advantage of you," Jake murmured softly, "I could very easily have done so. I didn't. I won't."

Caitlin closed her eyes, struggling for composure as his hand covered hers again, the beating pulse in her throat making it difficult to breathe.

How to explain to Jake that maybe she could trust him, but she wasn't sure about herself? His touch was turning her bones to water, the very sight of him making her forget every other man she had ever thought attractive. And, then there was Jenny...

She looked up at him at last, not quite able to meet his gaze. "It sounds so practical...but..."

Jake let go of her hand. "Of course, I don't want you to do something you're not comfortable with. I just thought it would solve your problem. Both our problems." He settled back against the leather banquette, shrugged as the waiter brought their salads.

He picked up the fork, said, "You know, Caitlin, perhaps it would be a good idea if you gave up the trip until Daniel can make it. No doubt, you're used to him taking charge..."

She glanced up, responding like a bull to a waving flag. An image of Daniel rose before her. Daniel greeting her with a knowing look on his face, telling her 'I told you so', never letting her forget she had failed in her stand against him.

"I am *not* going home," she said.

"No?" She thought she saw something leap in his eyes. "What *are* you going to do, Caitlin Harris?"

She glared at him. "I am going to see Italy as I planned."

"Oh?" said Jake. "How are you going to accomplish that, Cait? Buses and trains can't take you to all the places you want to see."

She gave him a long, warning look. "I'm going with you," she said, a slight tremulous quality in her voice betraying her ambivalence.

Jake's hand came out in a lightning speed thrust. "Let's shake on it."

She put her slender hand in his large one, noting the way it swallowed up hers, then withdrew it to tackle her salad.

Excitement kept her from swallowing and finally she put down her fork only to pick it back up and wave it at him.

"There will be absolutely no…no.."

"No, what?" said Jake, all innocence, his mouth pursed as if he were having a hard time not smiling.

"Oh, eat your salad," she commanded and reached for her wine.

But Jake was to have the last word. "If," he said, "you mean that there will be no 'fooling around' or whatever they term amoral behavior these days, you're right. We're both engaged to other people."

He smiled at her. "You, Caitlin Harris, are as upright as they come. It couldn't be plainer if you wore a sign on your forehead. Being the sterling character that you are, you will not try to usurp Jenny's place in my-uh-affections. Granted?"

She smiled back, affirming it.

"As for me.." Jake paused as if he were trying to choose the right words. "I accept and appreciate the fact that you love Daniel, that you are at the moment annoyed with him and eventually, after you whip him into shape, are going to marry him."

"I was raised," he continued, "to behave in an honorable manner in all things but especially where young ladies were concerned. I do not take advantage of a vulnerable, possibly lonely, woman who is temporarily on the outs with her fiancé."

Jake stopped and downed his wine in one gulp, before concluding in a slow, deliberate manner, "Nor do I take advantage of your fiancé who is absent, and therefore, unable to protect his claim."

She wanted Jake to stop going on in this fashion, to tell him that any relationship with Daniel was now impossible—not after she had met Jake. Jake was off limits and she couldn't have him, but his kindness and attentiveness after the early brashness, had been so remarkable that she could never settle for someone of Daniel's ilk again.

They left the Fiorito the next morning but only after Marisa had taken a photo of Jake and Caitlin in front of the hotel with Caitlin's camera while Tina and Signora DeLuca watched.

Jake hammed it up, pointing out with one hand the Stetson which he had retrieved from the car and stuck on the back of his head. With the other he pointed to his tooled boots.

"Proof for the Texarkana gang," he told Caitlin. He grinned, then placed the Stetson on Caitlin's head and directed Marisa to take another shot.

.   After saying goodbye to the DeLucas, Caitlin shoved the camera back in her handbag, and they were on their way.

Past San Margherita, they were up and on the Autostrada in almost no time. High above the Mediterranean, the view was spectacular. Jake pointed out Genoa as they passed the historic site, and Caitlin mourned the fact that she hadn't been able to tour the city when she picked up her rental car.

"You'll just have to come again," Jake said in a soothing manner. "Maybe several times. You know that four-fifths of the world's art is in Italy. And you certainly can't see it all in one shot, much less the whole country. And don't forget Sardinia and Sicily and…"

"I know, I know," said Caitlin who'd pored over the travel books in planning her honeymoon. "All this trip is going to do is whet my appetite for more." She sighed with satisfaction and settled back to enjoy quaint mountain villages punctuated with steepled churches high on the right and always the shimmering, brilliant azure sea on the left below, a sight that left her gasping with its beauty.

They had not gone far when they passed through their first tunnel, an engineering feat that inspired awe and some unease. Jake explained that Italian engineers thought it more efficient to go through the mountains than around them. "There'll be a lot more before we get to Monaco."

There were 144 dimly lit tunnels —give or take a couple. Caitlin tried counting them but lost track. Some were short, some extra long, and it was in the latter that she held her breath waiting for the first glimpse of sunlight. Jake sensed her anxiety and reached over to pat her knee. "I'm going well below the 120 speed limit."

Knowing that he was talking kilometers did nothing to assuage her anxiety. It was the other drivers she was worried about. Europeans seemed fearless, but she had read about multiple car pileups.

In between the tunnels she admired the flower plantations on the terraced hillsides above which gave this part of the Riviera the name, Cote d'Fiori. The tunnels behind them, Caitlin gasped in terror as Jake began negotiating the staggering hairpin turns that led down to the gleaming ribbon of sand and sparkling sea bordering the tiny principality of Monaco.

The Cote d'Azur was aptly named, Caitlin observed, trying not to pay attention to the dangerous curves, focusing instead on the glittering water below. "And to think Daniel preferred a conference to all this," she murmured to herself.

"He always was an ass ," Jake returned and when she stared at him, added quickly, "From what you tell me."

A sudden twist in the road, the worst yet, had her sucking in her breath.. "Relax. I've driven these roads before, and they're not as dangerous as they look. Keep an eye open for the royal palace. It's pink and square and built on a rock."

At last they made it down to the waterfront where they parked and then walked along the esplanade. Choosing a place to eat was a simple matter. Jake found a small shop that quickly put together a portable lunch with cold roast chicken, fresh rolls, mixed fruit that Italians called Macedonia and a small bottle of chilled wine. He drove them to a large parking area fronting on the water and put down the convertible top. Pouring wine into paper cups, he suggested a toast.

"To the Riviera, to a trip full of wonderful sights and adventure, to us, partners in adversity." Caitlin sipped, then drank thirstily, aware that she had never been happier, and was more alive than she had ever been in her life. With effort she tamped down the niggling anxiety that tried to break through her present state of mind.

Afterward, Jake drove about pointing out the casino and the Gran Prix route that snaked through the principality.

"Are you a gambler?" he asked, smiling.

Caitlin shot him a look. "I must be. I'm with you aren't I?"

Jake's eyes sparkled. "Stick with me, kid," he said in his best Bogart imitation. "Together we can't lose."

His words, the tone and the look in his eyes touched off an alarm system in Caitlin's head that made her mind spin. For the next week and a half she would be casting her lot with a man she barely knew, a man who took silly dares and said outrageous things, a man who, furthermore, had the proven ability to keep her off balance.

A shiver went through her. *How could she, Caitlin Harris, be doing such an un-Cait-like thing?*

Chapter 4

Instead of returning to the Autostrada to complete the last leg of the day's journey up the Riviera, Jake chose to take the shore road from Monaco to Nice. It was a short distance, and Caitlin was grateful to avoid any more of the hairpin turns by which they'd earlier descended into the small principality.

Parking the Mercedes near the large harbor, they got out to better admire the yachts and the luxury hotels lining the waterfront. The sun was brilliant overhead, the sky a cloudless blue.

"My first French city!" Caitlin said in satisfaction, thinking one more time of how she had narrowly missed seeing this part of the world. On the wide tree-lined avenue behind them were huge chateaus set in magnificent gardens and bordered with ornate iron fences.

"Nice is nice," Jake punned and was rewarded with a resigned shake of the head and a smile that Caitlin could not hold back. She was becoming accustomed to his particular brand of humor and thought again how much it revealed about him. His sense of the ridiculous and his ability to poke fun at himself was not only a sign of supreme confidence, but of a quick wit. Was there anything sexier than intelligence? Life with Jake Riordan would never be boring, she mused, and added, lucky Jenny, before she caught herself.

The inn where she was staying was on the far side of the city and upon reaching it, Caitlin let out a long breath of pleasure.

Another converted residence with long green lawns that swept down to the brilliant sea, Maison sur La Mer satisfied all Caitlin's fantasies of what a villa in the south of France should be.

The scene Caitlin half feared at the registration desk never materialized. The young woman in charge greeted them pleasantly and found nothing amiss in the fact that she and Jake had different last names. But then the French had always been more liberal in their thinking, less rigid when it came to relationships. And, then, as Jake had pointed out, so many business colleagues traveled together, there was nothing remarkable about their joint occupation of the rooms. Even married people, Caitlin realized, sometimes had different names, the women retaining their original surnames.

Summoning a bell boy to take their luggage, the clerk explained that their suite was in the smaller, second structure linked to the main villa by a trellised walkway, lush with glossy greenery and colorful, fragrant pink and red blossoms.

Silvery gray with salmon pink shutters and mansard roof, the dwelling beckoned invitingly. According to the clerk it had once been the sizeable guest house on the original estate. "It has only been recently remodeled, and I think you will enjoy the ambiance. Enjoy your stay," she added.

Their suite, off a small hall, was on the first floor facing the sea. Spacious with French doors opening on to the lawns and the water beyond, the two bed-sitting rooms were all light and air. Caitlin noted with relief that each had its own bathroom.

Delicate blue and white figured wallpaper, repeated in the rooms' fabric, provided a charming backdrop for the brass beds, white wicker chaise longues and bedside tables.

The larger of the two rooms was equipped with a graceful desk and white and gold telephone. Spotting it, Caitlin unwittingly conjured up a vision of Daniel making trans-Atlantic calls to keep tabs on his insurance empire.

The connecting door between the two rooms was without a key and Caitlin's gaze focused on it until she realized Jake was watching her with amusement.

She shifted her gaze and went to the French doors of the second room and opened them to view the park-like surroundings and the sea beyond.

Jake tipped the bellboy and came to stand behind her. "It's something else, isn't it?" he murmured. His breath was warm on the nape of her neck and a spiral of excitement coursed through followed by an immediate warning from her over sensitized brain: Jake is taken, Jake belongs to someone else.

Caitlin turned around, ostensibly to inspect the rooms a second time but with the underlying purpose of short-circuiting the sensation. Studying a Monet print hung over the bed, she asked without looking at him, "Any preference as to rooms?"

He shook his head, his gaze still full of amusement as if he knew just what she was going through. "I'm here on your forbearance, remember?" He looked around the room. "They look pretty much the same to me."

"Take the one with the desk, then," she offered, "You might need to use it for business." And then remembering the stated purpose of his trip, "Are there any hotels in the area that you might be considering?"

He paused, said over his shoulder, "As a matter of fact I do have a lead on one just north of the city. Have to do some further checking before going there. Taken a look at the bathrooms yet?"

"I was just about to." She couldn't imagine them being anything but suitable adjoining the charming bedrooms. She moved over the cool tiled floor to the door off the second bedroom and snapped on the light. "A couple of notches up from the one at the Fiorito," she called out. Peach and ivory tiles covered the walls and floor, and the large modern tub and thick towels were more than inviting.

"I'm a little disappointed in the mirror though," she said, trying to cover the anxious qualms that bedeviled her as Jake joined her in the narrow bathroom.

"Why's that?"

She surveyed the full length reflection of the two of them on the mirrored wall opposite the tub. "It's not distorted or wavy. This one may be too accurate."

"I'm sure you have nothing to be concerned about—with or without clothing," Jake said. Caitlin closed her mouth on a retort. To chastise Jake for his outrageous remarks was to encourage him. She'd learned that much at least. To hide her warm cheeks, she moved to the door, and looked behind it to find a peach-colored terrycloth robe

"Nice touch." Jake reached out to examine it, taking the material between two fingers. "Nothing but the best for guests of Le Maison sur La Mer. Perhaps…"

"Perhaps what?" Caitlin asked over her shoulder as she moved from the small, compromising space.

"I was just thinking," he said from the doorway, "that robes might be one of the extras we start incorporating at our inns. It's this kind of amenity which helps set us apart from the big hotels. Very few do it—other than for their frequent clients."

"Awfully tempting to pack one when you leave, though," Caitlin murmured. "What if a customer just happens to misplace one in his or her luggage on the way out?"

Jake shook his head in exaggerated distress. "*Ma-dom,* we do not have customers, only guests. Delightful, charming, upstanding citizens, every one."

Caitlin grinned. "Okay, so what if one of your delightful, upstanding guests decides to snitch one?"

Jake's eyebrows knit in deviltry, making her wonder what he had looked like as a young boy. Irresistible, she decided. That thought immediately leaped to a conjuring up what Jake's own little boys might look like some day. She averted her gaze in fear he was again reading her mind, but Jake was still back with the robe problem. "I'll think of something. Perhaps a beeping device sewn inconspicuously into the hem that would go off when the robe left our premises," he joked.

She shook her head, her thoughts on Jake's future children. There was no doubt they'd be full of mischief. Shining brown hair the color of glossy chestnuts, the girls in braids tied with plaid bows, and the boys with unruly locks falling over their foreheads. Deep blue eyes and mouths that loved to laugh...

Caitlin had often tried to imagine what Daniel's offspring might look like. The images she conjured up were always faceless: Boys, all of them, dressed in prep school shirts and ties, immaculately neat. They did not have faces, just blurs where the features should be.

Jake left the bathroom and tried her bed, sitting on it, nodding approval at both the firmness of the mattress and the density of the pillow. From there he strode to the closet to laud the extra pillows and blanket on the shelf above. He switched on the bedside lamp and frowned. "Not strong enough for reading, but whether it's a matter of wiring or because they believe the occupants will spend most of their time outside, is the question." He sat down once again on the bed.

Caitlin's insides did a somersault. The sight of him so at ease in her bedroom, on her bed, made her wonder what it would have been like if this had been their honeymoon, hers and Jake's. A suffocating feeling constricted her chest and cut off her breathing. She turned away so he could not guess the trend of her thoughts.

Once more Jake appeared not to have employed his mind-reading skills.

"How does a glass of wine on the terrace sound?"

"Oh, yes, " she answered, not yet covered from her overwhelming vision. "Just give me a couple of minutes."

"Ten minutes, all right?" And without waiting for an answer went into the second bedroom, pulling the door closed after him.

He hailed her a short time later from a white round table under a striped umbrella and as she approached got up to pull out her chair beating a white-coated waiter to it by seconds. There were half a dozen other tables on the terrace, but only one other occupied, an older man and a woman young enough to be his daughter, or even granddaughter. It was clear she wasn't by the coquettish smiles and toss of her head, her flirtatious manner evident even from a distance.

Jake paid no attention to them, but focused on Caitlin, surveying the flowered cotton skirt and pastel knit top closely. "You changed. Some of the new duds you bought in San Margherita? Very nice."

She nodded, pleased that he had noticed, happy that he approved. She sighed as she took in her surroundings. The terrace steps led to the green lush lawns which met the beach, some distance away. There were families playing in the surf, some older couples in beach chairs lined up in a row near the water and still others walking about the lush, spacious grounds. People enjoying themselves in a lovely setting. Again, she thought how close she had come to not experiencing it all.

"White wine, all right?"

"What?" She turned around to see Jake smiling at her. "Fine."

She'd be back in Connecticut where it was still damp and cold. Had she not come, she would have been brooding about the wedding which didn't take place, wondering what lay ahead for her and Daniel. The cancellation of the ceremony had been a matter of having Daniel's secretary notify the few friends who had been invited. If his family had been surprised, she did not hear about it, and Caitlin's family took it in stride as they had twice before. Thank goodness it was to have been a very small wedding with her sister Liz standing up with her, Daniel's father, who was also his business associate, his best man.

Daniel had convinced her that a formal wedding was not in their best interests, that a small ceremony in front of her pastor would take care of it. No elaborate white gown, just the long emerald silk dress she had worn as maid of honor in her sister's wedding.

She hadn't cared when Daniel broached the subject of a small wedding, not after it had been put off twice before. Maybe, just maybe, she had put up no objections because inside she knew it wasn't going to happen, that some urgent business matter would delay it once again. Or maybe it was because she had always believed that the most important part of a wedding was what came after the big day and the honeymoon.

"Caitlin?" Jake was gazing at her as if he knew she had been thousands of miles away. A slight breeze ruffled her hair, blowing a strand against her cheek. Before she had a chance to brush it back, Jake had done so, long fingers resting on her face for a fraction of a moment, causing her heart to quicken.

"Poppy gold," he said.

"What?" She was beginning to sound like an idiot.

"California poppies. Haven't you ever seen them? Same color as your hair"

"Oh?" she responded, unreasonably pleased and tucked the comment away, only vaguely aware that she was hoarding Jake's compliments for a rainy day—in this case the day they would part company,.

Caitlin thought few men were as extravagant with their compliments. If she were honest with herself, she reveled in them, though determined not to let his words go to her head. She had no doubt he'd been a lady killer since age four. The total opposite of Daniel. Still Jake's sincerity came through. Caitlin had no doubt that with the right provocation he could also cut her up into little pieces as he had that first morning in the Fiorito's breakfast room. And God forbid anybody ever make him really angry. The tongue lashing for that unhappy recipient was something she didn't care to think about .

She sighed. How was she going to spend so much time with Jake Riordan and not be swept away by her emotions? She must steel herself against his charm.

What are you planning this afternoon?" Jake asked.

" The beach. The water looks so inviting ." She looked at him. "Oh, but you don't have to worry about me. After all we needn't be in each other's pockets all day, every day. It's not as if we were…"

"Honeymooning," Jake finished for her.

She shrugged, not wanting to trust her voice. The truth was that she felt as if she were on a wedding trip. After all she had planned the itinerary as such, and if the man across from her was not the one who should have been there, she was hardly at fault.

"What about you?" Caitlin asked Jake in an attempt to break off her train of thought.

"I've a couple of errands."

"The hotel you mentioned?"

He nodded. "And a friend who is in town for the holiday. I'll pay a quick call."

Caitlin looked up, curiosity consuming her. She could tell nothing by Jake's face, but some instinct told her the friend was a female. Ridiculous, but she felt betrayed and had to admonish herself. Jake already belonged to Jenny. Caitlin had no business feeling possessive where he was concerned.

They finished their drinks, diversion provided by a young couple with two little ones headed for the beach. Weighed down with sand buckets, buoyant plastic animals and beach blankets, the parents were hard pressed to keep up with the children, who were babbling excitedly in their native tongue.

Caitlin watched Jake's face break into smiles as the rambunctious youngsters, a towheaded boy of 4 or 5 and his lookalike toddler sister, all but fell over their own feet in their eagerness to reach the sea, their Gallic accents drifting back up to the terrace.

"Nice place to bring a family," Jake murmured. Caitlin nodded, biting back a question to which she already knew the answer. Jake would want children, lots of them.

Daniel, on the other hand, when she brought the question up, seemed stuck. One possibly, if it were a boy. Daniel himself had been an only child. Knew nothing about sibling rivalries, about sharing or family solidarity. True, he and his father were close, his mother having flown the coop long ago and now living in Florida with a man ten years her junior.

Jake drained his glass. "Time to get a move on. Sure you're going to be all right? He surveyed the hotel guests on the lawn , then focused on those on the beach. It was clear when he turned back to her he had deemed them unlikely to pose any threat to Caitlin. She smiled to herself. If she didn't know better, it would seem as if Jake had designated himself her protector..

He left after telling her he'd return in plenty of time for them to go in search of the best French cuisine. Caitlin lingered at the table a while longer before going back to her room to change into the new two-piece swim suit she had bought in San Margherita. Donning a gauzy cover-up she locked the door and started down the lawn to the water, putting on her sunglasses as she neared the water. The beach was not sandy but filled with small stones. In some places, sand, where it did not occur naturally, was trucked in along the coast, she knew, but not here.

There were several beach chairs not in use and putting down a towel, she went to test the water.

"Is *fantastico*. Are you coming in?" The speaker, a young man she guessed to be barely 20 years of age with curly black hair, soulful dark eyes and a splendid physique was beckoning to her. His slightly accented English identified him as Italian.

"Not just yet," she called and found herself returning his boyish smile. He nodded, waved and waded over to a woman, perhaps a year older and began splashing her gently. Their similar dark good looks made her guess sister and brother, possibly cousins.

From her beach chair, hidden behind the sunglasses, Caitlin watched as the young woman half-heartedly splashed back, her gaze roving the water and beach as if looking for something more exciting. A cry attracted Caitlin's attention. One of the youngsters she and Jake had seen earlier had lost his hold on a toy sailboat which was now headed out to sea. She watched the young man go rescue it and present it to the little boy, then closed her eyes, soaking up the sun and breeze.

Peace overtook her and she had half drifted off when something hit her foot. She sat up abruptly, watching the two Italians run toward her and only then saw a Frisbee at the foot of her chair

"*Scusi.* Many pardons." The young woman came toward Caitlin and picked up the Frisbee. Dark curling hair hugged her well shaped head like a cap. She focused on the unopened book Caitlin had next to her and smiled.

"It is too sunny to read. Wouldn't you rather join us in the water? It would make Nico very happy. She looked back at the young man. My brother thinks you are very attractive."

"What are you up to, Francesca?" called the young man striding toward them, taking the Frisbee from his sister's hand. Then to Caitlin, " I hope you were not harmed."

"Not at all," Caitlin said smiling.

"You are staying here…?" Francesca blurted, then stopped. "Excuse me. Let me introduce us. I am Francesca Carli. This is my brother Niccolo. We are here from Milan, enjoying a few days. You are staying here at the hotel?" she asked again.

"Yes, we, uh, I arrived this afternoon."

"We?" Two pairs of liquid eyes brimmed with curiosity.

"A friend and myself."

"The man you were sitting on the terrace with earlier?" Francesca persisted.

"Yes."

"Oh, he is very handsome, very *maschile*…, manly…He is not here?"

"He has some business to attend to," Caitlin said in a cool tone, beginning to react to the interrogation.

"Francesca!" Her brother turned to Caitlin. "Please forgive us for being intrusive. We, too, are staying at Le Maison. The weather this time of year in Milan is not quite as mild, and we came for a few days respite from university. There is not a lot to do here in the daytime except soak up the sun. Please forgive my sister's, how do you say it, inquisition.

He was on the right track, she thought. Inquisitive nature and then some characterized his sister. Francesca. Caitlin smiled at him, impressed with the pair's fluency in English.

Emboldened, Niccolo Carli stuck out his hand. "And you, are you enjoying the climate, Signorina....?"

Caitlin shook hands, disarmed by the friendliness. "Caitlin Harris. Yes, this is a far cry from April in New England. It is a pleasure to meet you both."

Francesca, her gaze on Caitlin's ringless fingers, asked, "And your fiancé, he is from New England too."

Caitlin was torn between setting the young woman straight and telling her to mind her own business. Her upright Connecticut character won out.

"We are not engaged."

"Just friends." Francesca's gaze was knowing.

"Business acquaintances," she corrected. "We are traveling together as a matter of convenience. I had car problems," she added and found herself explaining how the rental car had met its demise.

"You are going to see more of France?"

"No, actually I am headed toward Milan the day after next before going on to Como."

"We are returning then too," exclaimed Francesca, and added, "If your friend, uh.. business acquaintance, has to stay on in Nice you could ride with us to Milan. He could pick you up there or meet you in Como. The train ride from Milan to Como is a short one."

Niccolo Carli shot his sister a knowing look, one intercepted by Caitlin. Francesca was man crazy, Caitlin decided. She guessed her age to be barely 21. Her brother, a year or so younger, was too immature to be let off the leash she decided. But the only one she was angry with was herself. When would she learn to be more discreet?

"Your plan sounds like a very practical one," the young man said.

"Perhaps it will lead to something more than a business arrangement," his sister added slyly.

"Unlikely," Caitlin broke in, and then added, "Actually Jake has someone back in the states and I," she fibbed, "have a fiancé waiting for me." Well, it was true, except she should have said ex-fiancé.

"How trusting you all are," Francesca murmured. "Italian men would not permit such a thing. Does your fiancé know of the arrangement?"

"He's very sure of me," Caitlin evaded and to put an end to the conversation got up and took the Frisbee out of Francesca's hand. "I thought you wanted some exercise."

They played energetically for a short time, then Caitlin declaring she wanted a swim, shucked her shirt and went in, taking delight in the warm water. She knew Nico's gaze was upon her and quickly she waded out until she could submerge herself to her shoulders.

The water was warm and soothing, but Caitlin took small pleasure in it, castigating herself for revealing anything about herself and Jake or their plans. She had to learn not to rise to the bait as she had with Francesca. The brother and sister played on until apparently they tired of the game or of each other's company. Caitlin could hear them bickering and shortly afterward they began wading toward the beach. Caitlin made the mistake of looking in their direction and saw Francesca waving in her direction, Nico looking on. She averted her gaze until she was sure they had disappeared into the hotel.

Caitlin followed not long after, looking forward to a shower in the tiled bathroom. She noted with relief that Jake was not yet back. She wanted privacy. Knowing that Jake was in the next room would not have let her relax.

The shower was brisk and refreshing and after washing her hair, a somewhat difficult process with the handheld hose, she donned the terrycloth robe and went to sit by the French doors to brush her hair dry.

A small yawn escaped her. A nap would be lovely and Jake probably wouldn't be back for some time. She stretched on the bed, and to her surprise felt herself drifting off.

Jake's entrance to his room via the hall did not awaken her, but his tap on their connecting door did. She sat upright abruptly as he opened it a crack and peered around it.

"Aha! Sleeping beauty. Good rest?"

She nodded, noting Jake looked as vigorous and vital as he had when they started off that morning from the Fiorito.

"Dinner? You haven't made any plans have you?"

"No, I haven't and dinner sounds terrific. The picnic lunch in Monaco was delightful, but I'll be ready for something more," Caitlin said. She smiled her pleasure at the thought of dinner with Jake. He had made no reference earlier to them being together for the evening. There had been the possibility he might return late from his afternoon appointment, and she had thought about inquiring as to the hotel restaurant offerings. Now she would not have to. And she was eager to see more of Nice.

"Take your time waking up. I'm headed for the shower. I see you've made good use of the hotel robe." Jake closed the door but not before letting his gaze rest briefly on her bare legs below the garment.

Jake might be engaged, Caitlin reflected, but that didn't prevent him from admiring other females, including Caitlin. The fact that he thought she was returning to Daniel didn't deter him either.

She wondered how he'd spent his afternoon. For some reason Caitlin was sure he'd been in the company of a woman. A young, attractive woman, whose Continental charms were much in evidence. The thought caused a spasm of jealousy—and then a spurt of anger—with herself. How stupid of her to conjure up such a vision. For all she knew his appointment had been with an aging, overweight Frenchman given to picking his teeth. The thought made her laugh.

"Enough woolgathering," she told herself and sprang into action. Not having a key to the door between the two rooms bothered her. There was nothing to keep Jake from walking in when he pleased. Thank goodness the bathroom door sported a lock.

She had unpacked earlier and now chose one of her new outfits purchased in the shop at San Margherita. A long silky cotton skirt in cream and rose was topped with a gauzy shirt. High heeled sandals completed the look. Her hair was already dry and the soft water had turned the gamin cut into a mass of curls. Too late to comb them out and besides she wasn't sure she wanted to. She noticed the effects of the sun the last couple of days had lightened it considerably. Poppy gold Jake had dubbed the color. California poppies. She'd have to look up a picture when she got home. Or maybe go to California and see them for herself. She was, she reminded herself, a free agent. Of course there was her shop to think about, but later in the year she might plan another trip with Antonietta holding the fort. The thought pleased her that she could make her own plans without consulting someone else.

Small silver shells at her ears and a medallion, hung from a fine chain, was her only adornment. The mirror over the dresser told her the outfit was becoming, a fact reinforced by Jake as he came back into her bedroom.

This time he knocked and waited until she pulled the door open. Clad only in trousers and a shirt wide open, his hair was no longer wavy, but as curly as Caitlin's own. His shoes and socks were in his hand.

Jake whistled softly. She started to blush as his gaze went over her. "Perfect but for one thing." As he had on a previous occasion, he moved toward her, his fingers on the top button. She felt his touch through the thin silk, and moved out his reach.

Her eyes, masked by sooty lashes focused downward, caught sight of Jake's bare feet. The intimacy of the moment was something she hadn't counted on.

Jake seemed to think nothing of it, and sitting on her bed, began pulling on his shoes and socks, listing the choice of restaurants. For a moment she couldn't breathe and she marveled that Jake was so nonchalant. Did he live a more liberal life style than she? Or was she far too naïve for this modern age?

Jake broke into her thoughts. "So what will it be? On the water or up in the hills and the particular pleasures of Provence?"

"Oh, the sea, please."

"Excellent choice. We'll try the hills tomorrow, perhaps. I think you'll like where we're going. Just give me a moment to call and see about reservations." He left without closing the door, and she could hear him on the phone a moment later, speaking in English, reminding her that once again she was in not only a very beautiful city, but a cosmopolitan one. The city of Nice, she'd discovered while planning the trip, had been founded by the Greeks and had likely become a resort under the Romans who'd built the extensive baths. Furthermore the Old Town was still very much

Italianate in flavor and a spot she'd hoped to explore. That was when it was to be Caitlin and Daniel traveling together. Things had certainly changed.

Not long after, they locked their doors and headed back to the lobby and then the car park. Caitlin spotted Nico Carli across the broad lawns just as he saw her. She returned his salute with a half wave, drawing Jake's attention.

"So you didn't sleep *all* the time I was gone," Jake murmured. Caitlin started to explain how she had met Nico and Francesca, about to downplay the interlude, when she met Jake's gaze. His even tone was at odds with the look in his eye. Had she not known better she would have identified it as jealousy or even anger. Quickly she changed the subject to the Roman baths and the Old Town, babbling on about the city's antiquity.

Jake said nothing, handing her into the Mercedes with dispatch, almost, but not quite, slamming the door. The leisurely drive along the *Promenade des Anglais* had her gasping with pleasure at the grand villas and gardens, but it was the *Vieille Ville* , the Old Town, which enchanted with narrow, winding streets and closely-packed red-tiled roofs. The Roman baths and amphitheater, home of the Nice Jazz Festival, had her making mental notes for her next trip. And there would be one, she vowed, suddenly eager to see all that she had missed of the world in her 26 years.

The restaurant Jake had chosen was, as promised, on the water. A deceptively rustic exterior gave way to dim lighting, tables covered in blue linen centered with white roses and candles flickering under crystal shades.

Their waiter—Caitlin had yet to see a female in the role except at the family-run Fiorito—was as self-important as those in Portofino and San Margherita, haughty in manner and garb. She and Jake chose their meal with care agreeing that half the charm of visiting a new spot was to sample the regional dishes and wine.

Having settled on the bouillabaisse, grilled turbot and mesclun salad, they settled back to enjoy the rose wine, the grapes grown in the vineyards of Beyond, another name for Provence Caitlin had learned. She took a sip.

"Okay?"

"Very much so," was the reply encompassing far more than her drink. Euphoria had taken hold dispelling any anxieties for the moment.

Jake's tan seemed even deeper against the pale blue of his dress shirt and navy jacket and Caitlin found herself wondering if he had sunbathed that afternoon with the mysterious friend. She would not ask him, of course, but she could inquire about his other mission.

"The hotel you were going to inspect. Any potential?"

"What? Oh, not really." His gaze had been intent upon her face as if he were studying the curve of her brow, the shape of her mouth.

"Wasted trip?" she continued, not wanting to dwell on that thought.

"Driving the byways of Nice can hardly be described as wasted."

Caitlin gave him a sidelong glance. If she didn't know better she'd think his purpose for this trip was just made up. But why should he pretend to be inspecting hotel properties if that were not the case? It didn't make sense. Unless she was missing something.

Jake raised his wine glass and moved it toward hers. The crystal caught the candlelight turning liquid blush into a magical potion. Their glasses clinked gently. "To an interesting two weeks— a partnership of mutual convenience," Jake intoned.

Caitlin sipped her wine as once again alarm bells went off in her head. This time Jake was reading her mind.

"No second thoughts?" he asked.

"What?"

"About coming to Europe on your own. Leaving your fiancé behind? You're teaching him a valuable lesson, no doubt."

Caitlin averted her gaze, debating again whether she should tell him it was over with Daniel. Letting Jake think she would return to the old relationship was a two-way safeguard. Jake would not think she was looking for a rebound romance, and if he thought Caitlin's emotions were tied up elsewhere, Jake would not feel guilty about traveling with her. Not that he seemed to think Jenny would be worried.

"No," she said at last. "No second thoughts."

"You're sure about that?"

"Very sure," she said and twirled the stem of the glass in her fingers. "Daniel definitely needs a lesson."

"What about the fax?"

"What about it?"

"Daniel must be worried to have sent it."

"If Daniel were the worrying type, he would have come with me." A note of annoyance crept into her voice. "Why are we talking about him, anyway?"

Jake shrugged. "Certainly not my choice of subjects on a starlit night on the coast of France with a beautiful companion."

Caitlin smiled. "Good." She let the compliment wash over her like a shower of blossoms.

At the far end of the dining room, someone began playing a piano. The lilting strains were picked up by a violinist who was moving through the room stopping now and then at a table.

Jake stood up and reached for her hand. Caitlin rose and let him lead her across the deep carpeting to the polished square of wood that served as the dance floor. When he drew her to him, it was as if she had been waiting all her life for this moment.

The music had an unreal, dream-like quality, and they moved slowly in their allotted space as more couples joined them. Jake's hand on the small of her back was warm, but he did not press her close, and for this she was grateful. The evening, the whole situation, was too heady as it was. She was more than ready to fall...Rebound, she thought. Common complication. She'd read enough about it.

Twice more during the drawn-out meal, Jake drew her to her feet. The second dance had been a fast number, and Jake had exhibited sure foot work. This last piece was an old French song with a haunting melody. Almost familiar. When Caitlin let out a contented sigh, Jake drew her closer. "Enjoying yourself?" he murmured.

"Need you ask?" The lights had dimmed further, the crowded dance floor slipping away with just the two of them in a world apart.

He hauled her closer yet to the danger of her composure and asked, "What's the refrain?"

It had come to her as he spoke, a movie theme, if she remembered correctly. "Love will not be denied," she translated, glad that at just that moment the music ended. Jake was looking down at her, an unsettling look in the dark blue eyes. He loosened his grasp for a moment only to gather her to him again. For one numbing moment, she felt his mouth on her hair, a touch so fleeting she was not sure she hadn't imagined it.

"Time to go?" he asked when she tried to stifle a yawn.

Her answer was a reluctant smile. She'd dance until morning if she weren't so tired.

The ride back along the shore road in the open convertible was mesmerizing, the moon's rays cutting a swath across the now black sea.

At their hotel, Jake parked the car and came around to help her out. His hand under her elbow, they walked across the lawn now wet with dew.

A ship, its outline twinkling with lights and anchored off shore, gleamed in the distance. Caitlin caught her breath. She had seen more beauty in the past several days than she had seen in a lifetime before.

She turned to Jake, looking up at him to share in the moment. He smiled down at her until the look in his eyes turned serious.

He took the key from his pocket as they approached their miniature villa. Once inside he preceded her to open the door leading to his room and ushered her in. The curtains at the French doors had been closed by the maid and without turning on the lights, he pulled them back and beckoned to her.

Caitlin moved toward him with the caution one might reserve for a mine field. He watched her progress and when she reached his side, he seemed to forget himself in the moment of ethereal beauty and curved an arm around her shoulders. They stood silently for a few seconds looking at the moonlit sea, Caitlin's senses awash. The splendor of the sparkling swath across the darkened water combined with the magic of Jake's touch had the effect of making her tremble.

Immediately aware of it, Jake turned her to him. "Are you all right? Is something troubling you?" The solicitous quiet of his voice only added to her quivering state.

She could not have answered if her life had depended on it and when he tilted her face up to look into her eyes, she shivered, increasing his concern. His gaze dropped to her mouth. .

"Cait, answer me."

She breathed in the scent of him, a fragrance quite apart from the aftershave and inexplicably her face was wet with tears for the beauty of the night, for what might have been. And this time she couldn't blame it on the wine. She'd had barely two glasses of the light rose.

"Cait, sweet Cait. Don't cry." His mouth on her temple, he dropped light, comforting kisses, moved down her cheek and...Caitlin's heart caught in her throat. She must push him away. But when his mouth found hers, she was helpless. She kissed him back, slowly, gently, the way he was kissing her. His kiss deepened. She followed his lead, responsive to every nuance.

Just when she thought her legs would no longer hold her up, his head lifted, his arms dropped to his side and he stepped back.

Bereft, she took a step toward him. But he was already murmuring apologies. His fault, it wouldn't happen again, he had no right....please would she forgive him.

Before she could find her voice, Jake pocketed the key he had earlier thrown on the table and strode from the room, muttering something about fresh air.

Caitlin turned and stared as the hall door closed behind him. With unsteady gait , she turned and went to her room.

Finding the light she sank upon the bed, her head in her hands. What had they done? Another week of this, sharing rooms with a man she was far too aware of, a man who already had a girl. It was insanity.

"Caitlin, you fool," she muttered, "you're playing Russian Roulette. A laugh, a half sob escaped her. "No," she amended, taking perverse pleasure in being exact. "You're playing Russian Roulette, Riviera style."

Chapter 5

Jake was out of sorts the next morning. Caitlin could not tell whether it was because another fax had arrived from Daniel or because Jake regretted the scene which had ended their beautiful evening.

She sipped her orange juice, eyeing him over the rim of her goblet. Caitlin, herself, felt marvelous having fallen asleep the night before as soon as her head hit the pillow. Jake had come in some time after and had left before she awoke. She had knocked on the connecting door after showering and dressing and when there had been no answer, had opened it. A rumpled bed testified that he had been there.

In the breakfast room in the main building, she found him glowering in a small alcove, his gaze on the long lawns and the sea beyond. She spotted the fax next to her plate and without looking at it , quickly thrust it into her handbag just as Jake looked up.

His gaze went from her purse to her face. "Not curious as to what the fiancé has to say?" His voice had an edge to it.

Caitlin shrugged. "It'll keep."

"He'll be phoning next."

"Not likely. There's the time difference and the conference he's conducting won't give him a moment to think about transatlantic calls." Caitlin knew Daniel all too well. Nothing interfered with work. Not even if his personal life had gone up in smoke. She turned to the waiter who had come with the coffee, grateful for the interruption.

Juice and croissant were all that she wanted, she told the waiter and saw that Jake, too, had settled for much the same. She looked at Jake. "Lovely morning," she murmured as if nothing had passed between them the night before."

"Yes." His gaze went over her, taking in the colorful cotton dress which bared her throat and her lightly tanned arms. It lingered for a moment at the v-neck and Caitlin felt her color heighten.

Jake drank his coffee, then offered, "I take it you slept well." She nodded. "I guessed as much, snoring the way you did half the night. The walls are remarkably thin for such a vintage structure."

"What! I did not snore," Caitlin protested. "I couldn't have. Nobody ever complained before..."

Jake raised his eyebrows. "Well, it isn't something a lover would mention, now is it?" He gestured toward her handbag as if Daniel were inside, not merely his fax.

"I...we...." She broke off.. . It was none of his business what she and Daniel had or had not done. "Liz and I went to New York last month to see a play and stayed overnight. She said nothing..."

"Liz probably snores too," came the rebuttal. "A family trait."

Caitlin scrunched her linen napkin into a ball, ready to throw it at him when she saw the dark look on his face. Though why he was dwelling on the degree of intimacy that had existed between her and Daniel was beyond her. It was almost as if Jake were a jealous rival.

She reflected that a description of her and Daniel's love life depended on one's interpretation of the phrase. It had been Caitlin who had engineered the first kiss—out of curiosity more than anything else. And it had been Caitlin who had ratcheted up the relationship.

Daniel's initial wooing was laced with something akin to passion . Later he behaved in the way he did with everything that was not related to business—expertly, efficiently, without involvement. Totally unsatisfactory. But she had thought that marriage would take care of that. His rare displays of affection after the first week or so had usually been made in public, their effect calculated. Caitlin realized at some point that she was responding with more enthusiasm than he and that had quelled any ardor on her part.

She stared out the bank of windows as Jake buried his nose in the International edition of the Herald Tribune. What had been the bond between her and Daniel? If there had been little physical attraction, there had been even less meeting of the minds. Daniel and she could not even agree on small matters, much less larger ones such as the importance of family or the need for the two of them to have time alone together.

Her reverie was broken by the sight of the Italians, Nico and Francesca Carli. Threading her way through the breakfast room, the latter moved in their direction, her brother following.

Before Caitlin could look away, Francesca had caught her gaze and waved and in another moment the pair was upon them forcing Caitlin to introduce them to Jake. They chatted for a moment, Jake restricting himself to the minimum courtesies although Caitlin noticed he missed nothing about the Italian girl's figure.

"Too bad you are sitting at a table for two. We might have shared breakfast together," Francesca said, pouting, never taking her gaze from Jake.

"Yes," said Jake without enthusiasm.

"Perhaps for lunch," Francesca persisted, but Jake interrupted her.

"We have a date with a friend in the hills. Enjoy your day," he told the brother and sister in a pleasant enough tone , but he was scowling at Nico.

"Very friendly," said Jake, his mouth pursed. "Good thing he left. He looked as if he was about to devour you for breakfast."

Caitlin shot him a cynical glance. As if Jake had not been doing the same to Nico's sister. "And what's this about a trip into the hills?"

"In a moment," Jake said, his gaze going back to her handbag. "You're not going to read the fax from your fiancé? It may require an answer."

He busied himself pouring more coffee for Caitlin and passing the basket of croissants.

Caitlin shrugged and took one of the warm rolls. "Daniel's messages never require answers. He merely commands."

Jake's eyebrows went up. "Perhaps you'd like to put him out of your mind for a while to explore other relationships." He turned his head, looking in the direction where the Carlis were seated.

Caitlin thrust out her jaw, but before she could think of a retort, Jake added, "It's quite possible Daniel may be flying over to join you. Since he's been sending faxes, he must have a copy of your itinerary."

Caitlin smiled. "If you knew Daniel, you'd realize how preposterous that sounds. If he couldn't tear himself away from the business for two weeks for a honeymoon, he's certainly not going to race over here just to assure himself I'm all right."

She buttered a bit of croissant, took a bite, then ran her tongue along her full lower lip to snare a minute drop of preserves. Jake stared at her mouth for a moment as if mesmerized before returning to his subject.

"Maybe Daniel's had second thoughts," he persisted. "It's silly not to open the damn thing. Unless," he said, "you're afraid of the contents."

"Oh, for heaven's sake!" Caitlin reached for her bag and grabbed the thin envelope from it, ripping it open with such vehemence she tore the paper inside. Piecing it together, she skimmed it. The message was terse, typical Daniel: *Concerned. Wire Assurances. Daniel.*

A smile tugged at her mouth. She was safe, though Daniel might not think so. She thought of the man across from her, the man who had kissed her the night before. If Daniel had any idea....

"What's so funny?" Jake growled.

Caitlin thrust the fax at him, waited until he read the three words of the message and then retrieved it and crushing it into a ball, tossed it to one side of the table as if it were a crumpled napkin.

She sipped her coffee, a sense of well being pervading her body. And why not? One man was sending frantic wires across the ocean, another sitting across from her sulking because of it. And a third man was more than eager to spend some time with her if the looks Nico had been sending her across the room were any indication.

She smiled at Jake across the table. "Perhaps I should change my mind and send Daniel word that not only am I safe, but that I am traveling in the company of...."

He did not let her finish "That's one way to get him over her posthaste." He studied her face. "If that's what you want...." Jake's gaze moved over her taking in the reddish gold hair, the gray-green eyes under sooty lashes, the way her dress defined her shape.

Caitlin put down her cup and put an end to the conjecture. "Well, it isn't...." adding, "I'm enjoying this taste of independence."

"And being footloose and fancy free?" Jake toyed with the keys to the Mercedes which he had taken from his pocket and placed on the table.

"Whatever that's supposed to mean."

"That until you return to the states, you are unencumbered, and should another relationship materialize, you'd have no problems with it."

"Is that the kind of person you think I am?" she asked, knowing quite well that he was referring to Nico Carli as a possible candidate and not himself.

Jake's voice was cool, as he glanced over to where the brother and sister were sitting. "You must know you're an attractive woman. Some people might call you beautiful."

"But not you?" The question was out before she could bite her tongue. Jake's smile was long, slow and maddening. "I should have thought what happened last night would have given you the answer."

The unexpectedness of his reply threw her and her cheeks grew warm remembering the kiss in the moonlight. . She had thought he wanted to forget it. It had been an accident. He'd made that clear. To cover her confusion she reached for the silver pot of coffee nearly knocking it over.

His hand covered hers as they both reached for it and together steadied the pot. "What's the matter, Caitlin? Skittish?" Jake asked.

Could he see her heart thumping under the fabric of her dress? She hoped he had not guessed how he affected her. Hadn't he told her to forget it, that it shouldn't have happened?

"You mean you wouldn't have kissed me if I had a wart on the end of my nose and my head was pointed?" Her laugh was brittle.

Jake laughed out loud, drawing the attention of the Northern Europeans seated next to them, a husband, wife and small daughter, all of them silver blondes and blue-eyed,

" I'm not sure there isn't a little point up there under your hair," Jake teased and pretended to study the top of her head..

Caitlin ignored the teasing. "About last night…" She looked him in the eye. "You said yourself it was an accident brought about by the wine and the moonlight. And I took it to be just that. It won't work otherwise, our staying in such close quarters…"

"Of course not," Jake soothed.

"And we will keep to a strictly business relationship?"

"Of course," he drawled. "We said we would, didn't we?" He met her gaze with a mocking one. We mustn't forget Daniel who's been sending frantic messages across the Atlantic. And then there's Jenny…"

Daniel and Jenny. The problem in a nutshell. Caitlin traced a pattern on the tablecloth with her little finger. Even if Jake were attracted to Caitlin, honor prevented him from doing anything about it. Jake was engaged to Jenny, the girl back home. Just because Jake and Jenny hadn't picked out a wedding date, didn't mean he wasn't serious about the commitment he'd made.

Caitlin had had several glasses of wine that night in San Margherita when he had told her about Jenny—Jenny who lived next door to his family, the girl Jake's mother was eager to have as a daughter-in-law. But wine or no wine, on the subject of Jenny, Caitlin's thinking was crystal clear.

But Jenny was only one part of the equation. Even if Jenny didn't exist, Jake would not make a move on Caitlin, she knew. Again it was a matter of honor. Jake thought Caitlin was still in love with Daniel, that in coming to Europe by herself she was merely teaching her fiancé a lesson. In Jake's eyes, Caitlin belonged to Daniel and eventually would go back to him. Jake's code of ethics would not allow him to steal a woman he thought was betrothed to another.

She would never go back to Daniel. Especially now that she had met Jake and discovered the kind of man she'd thought no longer existed. But she wouldn't tell Jake that she and Daniel were finished. If she did, it would look as if she were angling for Jake. Off with the old and on with the new. He'd think she was man hungry, just out to see how many scalps she could attach to her belt.

She looked up to find Jake surveying her, a quizzical light in his blue eyes. "Let's not make too much out of a simple kiss," he said, and she colored knowing he'd read her mind once more.

The trouble was it hadn't been a simple kiss—at least not for her. It had been proof that she was not immune to Jake's charm and irrefutable evidence that Daniel, if he ever meant anything to her, no longer did. But most important the kiss had demonstrated that unless Caitlin exercised strict control she would be, honor or no honor, in deep water, and soon.

"That goes without saying," she said and reaching for her bag, she rose, waved to the Carli siblings who were watching them and headed for the terrace.

Jake was right behind her. "Anything special you want to do today?" His breath tickled her ear, disconcerting her. He seemed to make it a habit of walking close to her, of speaking in an intimate manner, much as if they were a honeymoon couple, or as if he was protecting her from any other advances.

"I thought you might like to see something of the area," Jake continued. "The Riviera was also the stamping grounds of the French impressionists. There are museums and galleries up and down the coast as well as in the hills, any one of which is worth a visit.

"I know," Caitlin said, intrigued. "I've been reading up on the area and according to my guide book it's difficult not to stumble across one."

"Shall we spend the morning in Nice, then, if you are agreeable we have an invitation to lunch in the hills."

"Sounds marvelous." Caitlin, strolling the broad green lawns toward the beach and water, asked, "At whose invitation?" Another woman friend of Jake's she wondered.

Jake smiled. "Claude Bruneau. I phoned him last night and when he learned we were traveling together insisted you come along."

"A native?"

"No, an American with Gallic roots who was lucky enough to make enough money to come back and live just outside the village where his grandfather and great-grandfather were born. Claude is in his fifties, has an eye for beauty and charms every woman he meets." He shot her a look. "I should think you two will get along like a house afire."

She mumbled something under her breath, but he caught the fact that she was annoyed.

"Now what did I say to get your dander up?"

She ignored him. Let him think she had nothing on her mind but attracting men. She moved forward at a galloping pace and when he finally caught up with her, she'd cooled down.

At Jake's suggestion they spent a leisurely morning strolling through the city's flower-bordered streets and driving down the most exclusive neighborhoods so Caitlin could glimpse the great villas with their formal gardens.

Jake pointed out the Old City with its rococo Opera House, the Roman arena where gladiators once fought, now the home of a jazz festival. From there to the Chagall Museum where the great canvasses depicting the Old Testament were a big attraction. It was closed. The Matisse Musee was next, housed in an orange 17th century palace set in formal gardens. It, too, was closed.

"No rhyme or reason as to schedule," Jake said. "The French seem to follow the Italians in this regard." Caitlin was disappointed but as Jake said, next trip.

It was a little past midday when they began their drive up to a village in the hills. High above the sea, the drive was lined with pink almond blossoms and fields of lavender leading to stone houses perched on the rocky cliff.

Jake entertained her by describing how local establishments were filled with valuable art, evidence that the area had once been the favorite haunt of the young impressionists. They had often paid for their meals with a canvas.

"It's easy to see why they chose this place to paint," Caitlin said, gasping at the view once more.

Pine, cypress and olive trees along with orange and lemon groves and the brilliance of the cobalt sky above and azure sea below took Caitlin's breath away. Oleander, lavender, roses and tulips vied for attention.

Jake parked the car at the foot of the steep, cobblestone incline that led to the village dating to medieval days. Near a large church, they stopped to look out to sea,..

"Quite a sight," Jake murmured.

"Like dying and going to heaven must be," Caitlin returned. "Do you suppose the people who live here ever take it for granted?"

"Can't imagine so."

Filled with galleries and shops, the village was a tourist's dream, and when Caitlin spotted a small water color of the very view they had just enjoyed, she picked it up. Executed by a young artist, or so she guessed, the painting was more than reasonable. "I'll buy this on the way back—a souvenir that will remind me always of this lovely place…"

"And of the man who accompanied you?" Jake wanted to know.

"But, of course, mon ami," she said effecting an accent and a nonchalant tone, "who else?"

"Getting pretty cheeky," her companion said. She answered with a self-satisfied nod. She was gaining confidence in the new, independent Caitlin.

Jake's eyebrows rose, but his only answer was to urge her on and up toward the home of his friend. At the end of a narrow lane overhung with trees and flowering bushes, they were met by Claude Bruneau.

A square, compact man wearing a loose peasant shirt over baggy cotton pants and sporting a shock of prematurely silver hair, he greeted them at his gate.

"I've been waiting for you," he said as he kissed first Caitlin and then Jake on both cheeks. "*Bienvenue.* Welcome."

"Come," he added, "you must be parched after the long climb up. We will sit in the garden and Martine will bring us some refreshment."

The Bruneau cottage, dating back to his grandfather's time, was a simple structure, but the garden was luxuriant and elaborate in design. "Claude's hobby, one of them," Jake explained.

"It's lovely," Caitlin murmured.

Claude cast an appraising look over her and smiled. "As are you, my dear," he said, "but then, Jake, my friend, you've always shown excellent taste in women."

Caitlin turned to Jake, waiting for him to clarify their situation and when he did not, murmured with just a note of asperity, "I'm afraid we've given you the wrong impression, m'sieur. We are merely acquaintances, new ones at that, traveling together to minimize some travel problems. But, it was so kind of you to include me in your invitation. What a lovely place to live, and to paint."

"You must call me Claude, and it is a pleasure to have you here," he said as he settled them at a small table under a grape arbor. "Yes, I am a fortunate man to come back to my family's home and keep occupied at what I love best in the world, especially after my wife died."

He broke off with, "Ah, here is Martine with the wine. She looks after me well." And taking a tray with a decanter and glasses from a girl, who appeared to be in her early twenties, he motioned her to sit with them. Martine shook her head and turned silently, a pronounced limp discernible as she began to walk away.

Claude's indulgent gaze followed her. "A childhood accident," he said. "It has made my Martine somewhat shy."

' The girl's sweet, rather plain face and lack of presence were compensated by a lush, firm figure evident even under the loose dress. Was it possible that Claude and Martine...? She looked at Jake and frowned. His face gave away nothing.

Caitlin's gaze swept back to Claude then to Martine who was just rounding the corner of the cottage and then once more to Jake. His eyes were dancing, his mouth pursed with laughter at her unspoken question.

Shaken, Caitlin reached for the small tumbler of wine that Claude had put before her and drank. Why there had to be nearly 40 years difference between their host and the young girl.

"Claude works in oils," said Jake, making conversation..

"Oh," said Caitlin without looking at either man, fearful that at any moment she would be shown pictures of a nude Martine standing in her foot tub, ala Degas.

"Landscapes of his garden, mostly, right, Claude," explained Jake, the gleam of deviltry in the blue eyes threatening to become full-fledged laughter.

"An occasional figure," Claude corrected him. "Martine with the baby." He pointed to an easel on the terrace, half hidden in the shadows of the cottage.

Caitlin looked up, then rose to go to the painting. There in soft blues and white, a transformed Martine, no longer ordinary of face, nursed an infant, the child's shock of hair black against the mother's pale full breast. Three-quarters completed, the painting had an ethereal quality, the young mother's expression, beatific.

"Catlin drew in her breath with pleasure, then turned to the artist. "It's wonderful," she murmured. "Magnificent."

"Thank you," Claude said, and raised his glass, not to Caitlin, but to the silent Martine who had appeared on the terrace and was now smiling shyly.

"Martine is my niece. Her mother looks after the infant, young Auguste, while Martine looks after me. Her husband, Henri, works on the docks. They can use the money."

"How convenient for all of you," said Caitlin and shot daggers at Jake who had chosen that moment to remove a non-existent pebble from his shoe. Bent over to hide the laughter that shook his large frame, he straightened after a moment, bland of face.

Caitlin was furious with Jake, furious with herself. If she were not careful, she'd be seeing sexual liaisons in every relationship. She was not unaware of the reason. Being with Jake kept her mind always on the subject. As if on cue, their host spoke.

"So, now," said Claude, "what is this arrangement between you two? That is if you have no qualms about revealing…" He settled back in his chair, the sharp black eyes missing nothing.

Jake shrugged, putting the burden on Caitlin. "Being the gentleman that I am, I will defer to my charming companion.. But for Caitlin, we would not be here. It was she who had the good sense to reserve hotel rooms at the height of the Easter season."

"But it is because Jake has a car that we were able to use the reservations," she added. Glaring at Jake as she did so, Caitlin launched into a brief account of her car being damaged and how she had been about to give up her dream of seeing the Riviera and the Italian lake country.

Claude broke in. "You don't mean you were traveling alone?"

Caitlin nodded, seeing no reason to fill in the details. To her chagrin she heard Jake begin to explain the circumstances of her solitary visit. " Her fiancé's loyalties were to his business," finished Jake.

Claude looked at Caitlin, admiration in his glance. This time his glass was lifted in her direction. "To you, Mademoiselle. I always admire independence in a woman." He drained his glass..

"And so you two met at Portofino and discovering that the chemistry was right…"

"Oh, no, nothing like that," broke in Caitlin. "A matter of convenience only. We both wanted to see the area. Jake had the car, I had the reservations."

A smile crossed the older man's face. "And so there is nothing romantic about the arrangement?"

"Absolutely nothing," Caitlin hastened to add. She thought she saw Jake give Claude a look, and the matter of their trip was abruptly dropped.

After an excellent salad served by a still quiet, but now smiling Martine, Claude asked if they'd like to inspect the garden. Delphinium in a gorgeous purplish blue predominated. His studio was the next stop where a small number of landscapes in varying stages of completion were propped.

Caitlin exclaimed over a small oil showing a corner of his flower garden with a hint of the sea below. Filled with glorious light and color, it confirmed the talent that had been unmistakable in the picture of Martine and the infant Auguste.

When Claude took it from the packing case on which it was perched and attempted to press it upon her, Caitlin protested. "I wasn't hinting. I couldn't. It's far too lovely and valuable."

Smiling, Claude turned and thrust it upon Jake saying, " I insist my dear. Perhaps it will inspire you to come back some day—with Jake, of course."

Jake took the picture for her, saying to Caitlin, "I warned you about the Bruneau charm." And then completely spoiling the effect Caitlin had tried to achieve earlier, threw his free arm about her shoulders giving her a small hug.

Claude beamed. "You make a lovely couple. Together you would produce beautiful *enfants*, like Martine's small Auguste." Caitlin blushed at the frank appraisal..The Frenchman's comment brought to mind the kiss she and Jake had shared the night before.

Flustered, she said as casually as she could manage. "Then you don't know about Jenny, the girl next door back in Connecticut? Jake is spoken for."

"And you," quizzed Jake abruptly, his smile stiff. "The fiancé you walked out on?"

Caitlin shrugged, hoping that was the end of it. But Claude exclaimed, " You wouldn't go back to a man who couldn't find time to marry or bring you on a honeymoon?"

Caitlin merely smiled not letting her vexation show. Claude took a cheroot from his shirt pocket, offered one to Jake. "Human nature being what it is, you and Jake will likely find the rules you have set to keep you apart, a fragile barrier." He lit Jake's cheroot, then his own, looked at Caitlin, "Yes?"

Caitlin sputtered, turned to Jake expecting him to refute the possibility just in time to see him give Claude another warning look. She bit down hard on her lower lip.

Too angry to speak, she gazed off into the distance and heard Jake thanking Claude for his hospitality, that it was time to go.

She added her thank you in a quiet voice, hardly able to wait until she could get Jake alone and give him a piece of her mind for not setting Claude straight.

But they had no more than shut Claude's front gate behind them before Jake addressed the issue. "I hope you're not taking any of Claude's talk to heart. He was just making conversation."

"Then why didn't you speak up?" She grew angrier by the moment. "Is it because you figure at some point, I'll throw myself at you?"

Jake took a last puff on the cheroot, made a face and tossed it down, grinding it under his foot. They walked a short distance before he answered.

" Hardly. But if I said I wouldn't find the prospect of making love to you very enticing, I'd be lying through my teeth."

Caitlin glared at him."But, you're too much of a gentleman to even consider it?"

"Well, no, sweetheart. That's something I've never been accused of."

"So you admit it."

"Admit what?"

"That's it been on your mind?"

"I said I was honorable, not some halo-ed saint." He took her by the elbow and began walking her down the hill to the car.

She broke loose and stared stonily at him. "Back in Portofino when you were telling me all the reasons why we should travel together, you assured me that this wouldn't be a problem."

"It doesn't have to be."

That brought her to a halt. "You have a fiancée back home."

"So do you. That makes us even."

"You don't seem too constrained by it."

He paused and she could almost see the wheels going around in his mind. "Jenny is a modern girl."

Caitlin wasn't sure what he meant by modern. She could guess. "Neither of you care anything about commitment?"

He glared at her. "You're a fine one to talk."

"I haven't done anything wrong."

"You walked out on Daniel."

"To prove to him I have a mind of my own." And to me, she added silently..

"Did it work?"

She shrugged. She didn't know. But, at least she wasn't engaged and on the make the way he and his Jenny were. "I know how you privileged people operate—no morals, no…"

Jake's face hardened. "You don't know anything about me Miss Self-Righteousness. Or Jenny. She's as upright as they come—without being a prig. At least we didn't go into an engagement with nothing in common."

Prig! She flinched at his implied characterization. "You think I did?"

"What was the attraction? Certainly not physical," Jake flung at her. "You and Daniel couldn't wait to get away from each other." They were shouting. People were stopping to look at them. Jake suddenly thrust Claude's small painting into Caitlin's arms, grabbed her elbow and propelled her to the Mercedes a short distance away.

Jake opened the car door, still holding on to her, and put Caitlin inside. He went around to the driver's side and got in. Instead of starting the motor, he ran his hand through his hair and turned to Caitlin. "I'm sorry."

Caitlin looked over at him, the truth in his accusations stinging her anew. "I am, too. It's just that hearing Claude say those things got under my skin."

"I know." He paused, studied the steering wheel, then looked up at her from under half closed lids. "The thing is, Sweet Cait, it's been on my mind, as well. I'm a very normal man with all the normal instincts. But there's Daniel and there's Jenny..."

His hand came out, covered hers. "We're good friends, aren't we, Caitlin?" he asked

She nodded.

'Good," he said his voice husky. "Let's not tie ourselves into knots over what might have been and enjoy what we have instead. A deal?"

"Deal," she replied, not acknowledging her sense of loss.

The ride back to the hotel was quiet. Caitlin lay back against the leather seat, letting the breeze from the sea blow through her hair and cool her brow as she studied the wonderful painting Claude Bruneau had given her. She couldn't believe it was hers.

"Amazing," she murmured as she studied the small masterpiece. Jake looked over at her and she smiled back at him aware that the day was something she wanted to cling to in her memories. If her heart ached for the fact that their time together was finite, no one would guess, Jake least of all.

Claude was wrong, Caitlin reflected. There would be nothing between Jake and Caitlin. Jake belonged to Jenny. And if, at times, his attitude toward his betrothed appeared cavalier, he wasn't about to give Jenny up for Caitlin.

Nor would Jake try to have his cake and eat it too. He had convinced her.

That Jake might try to use her was the thing Caitlin had feared most. She had addressed that fear, dispelled it. She shot a sidelong glance at Jake, taking pleasure as always in the striking profile, the lean competent hands on the wheel, the elegant shoulders. All she need do was wait for the residual wave of regret to vanish.

Chapter 6

Caitlin fought to stay awake as Jake drove back to the city and through the streets of Nice to their seaside hotel. The return trip was taking longer than going had, thanks to a late afternoon traffic rush. Jake seemed to be handling it without undue stress. She glanced over at him, received a warm smile in return.

It was strange, she reflected, how a man whose only declaration had been of friendship could convey so much feeling, while a man who had professed love, publicly and privately, had convinced her of nothing. Her eyelids fluttered and closed.

Jake woke her in the hotel parking lot. It was getting to be a habit, falling asleep while in his company. He looked down at her, his mouth curving. "Wine, the great restorative."

"Or knockout punch, depending on your viewpoint," she countered, amazed she felt so relaxed with him that she could drop off like that.

"Now you're all rested for dinner. Where shall we go? Back to the hills or on the water?" Jake, himself, seemed to possess unflagging energy.

They climbed from the car. "You decide." Jake's choices on the trip had been excellent, including this afternoon. "Thanks for taking me to Claude's. I'd never have had the opportunity to visit in someone's home, had it not been for you."

"The pleasure was all mine. And Claude's. And his shapely housekeeper's." Jake's amused smile left no doubt that he'd known what Caitlin was thinking about Claude and Martine.

Caitlin protested. "It was the way he was looking at her."

"Tsk, Tsk," Jake teased. "Can't you tell the difference between a purely avuncular glance and a lustful one? Sometimes, sweet Cait, your naiveté surprises me."

"Oh, go jump in the lake," she retorted and walked off toward the hotel office.

"Sea. The Mediterranean is still a sea. At least it was this morning." Catching up with her, Jake threw an arm about her shoulders giving her a quick hug. "Purely avuncular," he assured her, laughing. She gave him a scathing look, and he jumped aside to avoid a well-aimed kick in the shins.

Caitlin went with him to the lobby. He asked for their keys and handed hers to her, murmuring something about an errand. She started out the door and down the steps to go to their smaller building, then remembered she'd seen a copy of the *International Herald Tribune* in the reading room next to the lobby and returned. Jake was at the front desk, his back to her, speaking to the concierge. Caitlin heard the word, fax.

Well, she reflected, that wasn't so strange. Jake was a businessman, too, if far less intense about it than Daniel. Earlier he'd said his brother took over when he was away. But no doubt he had to stay in touch with him while out of the country.

The fax she had received that morning from Daniel had not set well with Jake, she mused. The way he'd carried on, you'd almost think he had some stake in putting Daniel's mind at ease. Well, Jake was a considerate man. Probably didn't like to see anyone worry.

An unwelcome thought leaped into her head. Jake wouldn't take it upon himself to wire Daniel! No, he couldn't. Sloane was a common name and she had never mentioned the company name...

In her room, Caitlin sank onto the chaise longue and glanced idly at the books she had placed on the low table next to it. Since that fateful day at the beach at Portofino, she had not so much as opened one. Every waking moment had been spent either in Jake's company or, she berated herself, thinking about him!

***

The office of Le Maison was cramped to say the least. Jake felt claustrophobic as he waited for the operator to put the call through to Paolo. Still, the cubicle afforded a privacy that Jake sorely needed, and he had been grateful when the concierge had offered to let him use the telephone there.

The concierge, a superior creature with long nose and thick glasses, had not blinked an eyelash when Jake had explained he could not use the phone in the suite. Because there was no key between their rooms, Jake could not be sure that Caitlin might not walk in on him in the middle of the conversation. Not that she was given to such interruptions. But it was something he must avoid at all costs. No one must know his real purpose for being in the area. Least of all, Caitlin. Jake doubted she would understand the motive behind his actions.

The operator's voice interrupted his thoughts. His party was on the line. Jake's greeting was brisk.

"Paolo, the situation is more complicated than we thought. I've sent a fax to the states. Perhaps you should call him as well. I can't chance it here."

Jake spoke for a few more moments, filling Paolo in on the itinerary, then hung up. He was seeking out the concierge to pay the charges so that it would not appear on the room bill, when he realized his omission. Damn! He was so caught up in this mess, he'd forgotten to ask about the hotel's grand opening. Well, he and Paolo would have to catch up later when he returned the Mercedes. They'd have a lot to talk about, that was for certain.

* * *

Jake's key in the hallway door to his room alerted Caitlin that he'd returned and a moment later he tapped on their connecting door, entering after she called out to him.

"Without hesitating, she asked if he'd sent a fax."

A look crossed his face, but was gone in a moment. "Yes, how did you know?"

"I remembered I'd seen the Tribune in the lounge earlier and wanted to borrow it. Someone had already taken it."

"Why didn't you say something?" Jake wanted to know. "I'd have asked the concierge to scare up another one."

"No problem." She glanced up at him. "Mission accomplished?"

"What?" he looked puzzled.

"The fax."

"Oh, yes, just a quick couple of lines to my brother Harry. I mentioned we were partners in the business, didn't I?"

Caitlin nodded.

"Figured I'd better keep in touch, let him know where I can be reached." Smoothly he changed the topic. "About dinner. How does a floating restaurant sound?"

"Wonderful. On ship?"

"Anchored off shore up the coast a few miles. Paolo mentioned it when I asked for suggestions."

She sat upright. "You phoned your friend in Rome? From the lobby?"

"From the office." He stared back, amused by her curiosity. "Why should that amaze you?"

She shrugged. Why would he call Paolo Cimino and why from the office and not the phone in his room?

Jake laughed. " I thought he was entitled to know from time to time where his car is. I was in the office to change some money and used the phone there while I was waiting." He dismissed the subject. "Now about dinner on the ship?"

"It's anchored off shore? How do we get to it?"

"How do you think? We swim, Ducky!"

The small chaise pillow Caitlin threw hit Jake between the shoulders as he beat a retreat. Unable to suppress a smile, she went to pick it up, eager for the evening to begin. Every outing with Jake was an adventure. She was glad she'd asked about the fax. So he'd wired his brother and let Paolo know where his car was. Understandable. She'd better watch herself. She was becoming paranoid. She didn't want anything to interfere with the rest of her trip—something she feared Daniel might engineer if his communiqués were answered.

She glanced at her watch, saw that she had plenty of time to get ready. Jake wanted to leave about 8, he'd said. The late hour that people preferred to dine in Italy and France still seemed strange.

She opened the French doors, stepped onto the terrace and gazed at the sea for a few appreciative minutes. She was just ready to head back in when she heard her name called. From a distance Francesca Carli, in a beach cover-up, was waving at her. She strolled across the grass to meet her.

"Where have you been all day?" Francesca pouted prettily. "Nico and I were looking for company." Caitlin smiled, realizing that the hotel was not exactly a singles haven. Couples, young ones with children, and older pairs seemed to outnumber the other guests. Francesca was looking at the French doors as if she were hoping Jake would appear.

"We spent the day visiting a friend ," Caitlin told the younger woman. "It's my first trip in this area, and we planned on making brief visits to the art centers. But they were closed. No doubt, you've been?"

Francesca laughed. "From birth. My parents are art collectors of a sort and my mother believes in early appreciation of the arts." She looked at Caitlin. "We go home tomorrow. What about you and your friend?"

The younger woman continued to scout the area even while she was talking.

Caitlin nodded. "We're headed for Milan and then Como. I hope the weather's like this."

"It won't be," Francesca moaned. "That's why we're here."

"But a lovely area?"

"Oh, yes," Francesca agreed. "There is nothing more beautiful than the Lake District. Ciao, have to go," she said abruptly and Caitlin watched her race to catch up with a blond Viking who had appeared on the lawn. Clearly, Francesca was man crazy.

A few moments later, Caitlin went back inside to decide on a dress for the evening. She came out of the shower, a short silk kimono over her underthings and was drying her hair when Jake tapped on her door. She opened it and he held out his hands, the cuffs of his half-opened dress shirt dangling. "Do the honors will you?" He held out a pair of gold links. "They're tricky to get in."

Standing in the doorway between their two rooms, she inserted the first link into the shirt cuff, dropping the other as she did so. They both went down at the same time to recover it, their heads almost colliding. She backed off too quickly as if he'd bite, last night's encounter in the moonlight very much in her thoughts. She couldn't chance another such occurrence.

Jake's voice filtered through. "Relax, Cait, just pretend we're an old married couple."

As if that thought would steady her nerves! She rose keeping her head down, avoiding his gaze, and accomplished the task.

"Thanks," she heard and felt, rather than heard, him move away from her. With a sigh of relief she heard the door close.

As it turned out, Caitlin required Jake's assistance as well. As she finished dressing, she slipped a silky dress over her head and in her still unsteady condition managed to jam the zipper six inches from the top. Gently she tugged, squeezed, maneuvered the zipper to no avail. Fearful of tearing the delicate fabric, she finally had to seek Jake's help but only after minutes of debating with herself. The triteness of the situation appalled her. Jake might construe it as a ploy. And after last night, she didn't want any semblance of intimacy to intrude.

Jake's cheerful grin as he opened the door to her knock dispelled her anxiety. "You see, we do need each other. Turn around." He moved into her room and taking her by the shoulders swiveled her around until her back was to him.

The touch of his hands on her upper arms through the thin silk unnerved her, but not half as much as his warm breath on her back did.

"There's a loose thread caught in the teeth," he diagnosed. " I need three hands. Two to keep the zipper parted and one to pull the thread. No, wait, I've got it," he exulted.

She could feel his hands on the zipper and then, incredibly, she felt his mouth warm on her back. An involuntary shudder went through her, a sensation so strong she placed a hand on the door frame to keep from falling.

"*What* ARE you *doing*?"

"WILL YOU HOLD STILL!! I almost had it," he moaned.

She whirled to face him and repeated her questions, her face and body flushed.

Jake explained his actions as if she were from outer space. "Getting the thread out with my teeth. What do you think I was doing? I saw my mother do it once—when I was a kid. I thought it was clever of her."

"On her own dress?" She must be a contortionist." Her voice was icy.

Jake stopped, disgusted as the full impact of the sarcasm hit him. "She'd managed to slide the blasted dress off. Now will you hold still or do you want to leave it and go the way you are?"

His threat helped to calm her. She turned around and once again felt his warm breath on her back, causing turmoil inside.

Then, "Success! I can pick out the rest of the thread by hand if you'll just relax." And as Caitlin stood quivering, Jake gently worked the zipper free, keeping up a running patter.

Jake's method of diverting her was to pretend they were long married and beset by a series of domestic crises. Their twelve-year-old son had just eloped with his piano teacher, the paranoid poodle was in need of a new analyst and the butler, on a caffeine high, had ambushed and shot the moose head over the mantel."

The result had her giggling by the time he finished freeing the zipper. Jake gently pulled up the mechanism and turned her around. Instead of letting her go, he appraised the picture she made from the poppy gold hair to the hem of the emerald silk that gently clung to her figure.

Jake's whistle made no noise. Silently he reached over to smooth a tendril of hair off her cheek. The look in his eye chased the laughter from both their faces.

Caitlin stared back. The white lawn shirt under the dark suit was a foil for the deep blue eyes, the shining chestnut hair. He took a step toward her and she quickly blurted. "I'm ready. Shall we go?"

"No shoes? That'll be interesting." Flustered she moved to the closet to slip on the high-heeled sandals. She'd never met anyone who could keep her so off balance as Jake could.

A motor launch took them to the floating supper club. Its plush décor lent a never-never quality to the dream world Caitlin was already living in. Her first impression was of brass rails, potted palms and crystal chandeliers. Lights from shore twinkled in the distance through an expanse of glass.

Caitlin followed the tuxedoed waiter across deep, silky rugs to a leather banquette. Jake was behind her. When they were seated, she turned to him, her eyes wide. "Hartford was never like this."

He grinned and began consulting the wine list. She heard him order, realized his French was far better than his Italian, thanks, perhaps to his being conversant with hotel and restaurant matters.

They consulted the menu. She shook her head over the many choices asking him to choose something simple for her. The dishes were far too elaborate with sauces and other embellishments.

Jake ordered and they sat back to listen to muted selections. The food came, beautifully cooked, artistically arranged--and delicious, no doubt. She pushed it around on her plate, letting the music wash over her. Jake reached for her hand, and without speaking, brought her to her feet. Her hand still in his, they moved to the small dance floor. Once again, the music and enchantment of the night washed over her as he took her in his arms.

Several times between the many courses, they got up to dance and in each instance she went into Jake's embrace as if it were the first dizzying time.

"Enjoying yourself ?" Jake's mouth was against her ear.

With difficulty she brought herself from the edge of the precipice.

Lifting her cheek from the softness of his lapel, she tried to thank him. "It's been a wonderful day. Exploring Nice, our foray into the hills, just seeing where the galleries are, so next time..."

"So when you come back with Daniel, you'll know just where you want to go..." There was an edge to Jake's voice.

Suddenly she was tired. Tired of this farce, of waltzing around in the arms of another woman's man. She stopped abruptly, pulled out of his arms, taking Jake by surprise.

"What's the matter? Want to go? We can have a nightcap here or we can move down the coast. There's a small café..."

"No," Caitlin told him. " My head is hurting. If I'm not cutting your evening short, I think I'd like to turn in early."

He stiffened. "I don't know what just happened, but there's no need to utilize the traditional wifely complaint. I've no intention of making a move, if that's what you worried about."

Her mouth in a tight line, she moved across the dance floor to their table. Picking up her wrap and bag, she headed for the door to an outer lounge to wait for him. It seemed forever before he appeared and she realized he was settling the bill. He had made it clear to her at the start of the trip that because she was paying for the rooms, he would take care of the meals.

When at last he found her, his face was grim. "Couldn't you have waited for me? Are you that eager to be out of my company?"

She didn't answer and they rode in silence in the motor launch back to the dock. When they were inside the car, Caitlin reached into her bag and pulled out some bills. "I'd like to pay for tonight's dinner. You did last night."

Jake swore under his breath.. "When I want you to pay, you'll be the first to know."

Caitlin thrust the money back in her bag and slid to the far side of the front seat, a move that drew another grim look from Jake. The tension grew, the moonlit drive back down the coast to their hotel ruined.

In the parking lot, she didn't wait for him to get out, but hurried from the car to the hotel lobby. Jake was right behind her. They reached the desk together, Jake's shoulders stiff, face taut, as he asked for their keys. Caitlin saw Nico Carli, resplendent in navy blazer and white slacks, approach. She dropped back from the desk, eager to avoid any confrontation between the two men.

"A pleasant evening?" Nico asked Caitlin.

"Yes," she murmured, then watched as Jake turned to see the two of them and frowned. He glared at Nico.

Quickly, Caitlin sought a safe subject. "You and your sister are returning home soon?"

"In the morning, very early," Nico confirmed. "And you and Signore Riordan?"

"We too leave sometime tomorrow. Jake sees no reason to hurry. He is planning a leisurely drive through the mountains."

"Signore Riordan decides the schedule, hmm?" Nico's gaze was warm and intent on her face.

Caitlin shrugged. "It's his car." She looked up to see Jake still at the busy desk waiting impatiently for the keys. He glared at the two of them and Nico seeing it, chuckled.

"I think you are mistaken about your convenient arrangement. Signore Riordan has put a stamp upon you." Nico's mouth curved. "No one else may even look at you or talk to you."

"That's not true," Caitlin snapped. Such forthright talk and from a stranger, yet, was more than a little annoying. In fact, the second stranger to draw such a conclusion within 12 hours. She felt like screaming.

"Oh, no?" Nico smiled as Jake, keys in hand, walked toward them. "I think Signorina, that *amore* will decide what is true and what is not.

"Not waiting to hear what Jake might say to Nico, she grabbed her key from Jake's hand as he neared, then fled.

Once in her room she headed straight for the bathroom. Trembling with anger and nerves, she ran a warm bath, the noise of the rushing water blocking out all sound.

She seemed to be always getting herself into the same situation. As she had that first night in San Margherita, Caitlin had been brought up short by being reminded of the Jenny problem. She hated the very name, the sound of it, the thought of the person who possessed it. Because that person also possessed Jake.

Caitlin was far from soothed when she climbed out of the cooling water. If anything she had only managed to work herself up more. Toweling herself off, she slipped on the peach-colored robe and began brushing her hair with punishing strokes.

In the mirror she caught her reflection. "Poppy gold," was how Jake had described her hair. "Beautiful Cait," he'd called her tonight. Words, mere words, all designed to break down her defenses.

She opened the door to the bedroom, her gaze going to the French doors, half opened, the draperies moving in the breeze. She hadn't opened it! Not until she was halfway across the room, did she see Jake outside, staring into the darkness.

"What is it? What are you doing here?" Her voice was weak.

He moved inside. "Sit down." He pointed to the bed. The imperious tone fed her simmering anger.

"I'm going to bed. I would like you to leave."

"After I've had my say."

"You've already said all I want to hear."

"But not from that young Romeo, still wet behind the ears. What did he have to say that was so interesting?"

Caitlin stared at him, temper making her indiscreet. "The same thing Claude said, the same thing the desk clerk thinks, what everybody is thinking—that our arrangement is all too chummy. That if we aren't already intimate, then it's just a matter of time until you persuade me to jump into bed."

"And you believe them? Did you ever stop to think, Caitlin, that your readiness to believe the worst about me may be wishful thinking. Maybe you'd like me to play the ardent lover. After all your fiancé refused to come with you on a honeymoon. Maybe your self-image is in need of bolstering…"

"Get…out…of my room!   Jake's answer was to move closer, and anger inflaming her, she rushed at him trying to dislodge him from his spot by pushing at him.

His lean bulk didn't budge, and furious, she lost control . She lashed out, one hand grazing his chin. He let her wear herself out and just as she was about to give up, he picked her up and dropped her on her bed, standing over her like some wrathful god.

Stunned by the ease with which he had lifted her, she croaked. "Go away!" and hid her face.

"Why should I? If I'm going to be accused of seduction, I don't care to be found wanting."

He came toward her, his intent all too clear. Frightened, she started to slide off the other side of the bed, but he caught her by one ankle. In an act of desperation, she curled into a ball, face down, a smaller animal protecting itself against a larger predatory one.

A loud humorless laugh filtered through to her ears. "What an easy target, but I'll have to forgo the satisfaction. Your parents should have warmed your backside years ago. Now look at me." Reluctantly she took her face out of the pillow.

"Get this straight, Caitlin Harris. I had no intentions of making a move on you, nor, and this may be more important, was I going to let you work your magic on me. I thought we both deserved better than some fly-by-night affair."

Her face burned and her body ached with embarrassment and chagrin.

"I hoped you would trust me," Jake added. "Instead you persist in listening to others who think our resolve is as spineless as theirs."

He backed away and she turned over, her gaze not quite meeting his.

"Tomorrow," he said, "I'll drive you to Milan and you can catch your train to Lake Como from there. You should have no trouble with public transportation for the last part of your trip." She heard the door close as he went to his room.

Chapter 7

Caitlin slept little that night, too conscious of the man in the room next to her. The finality of his words and the bitter tone tore at her.

Long before dawn she awoke, packed, then washed and dressed quietly, fearful any sounds she might make would filter through to the next room. If only she had a telephone so that she might call Nico and Francesca Carli. Last night she had decided she would not impose upon Jake Riordan for a moment longer than necessary.

The wish for a fast means of getting to Milan where she could catch a train to Lake Como had no sooner formed in her mind than she remembered Francesca's words that first day on the beach. The invitation to drive to Milan had not been seriously tendered, its purpose in Francesca's mind to get to know Jake better. But Caitlin thought it likely the brother and sister wouldn't mind giving her a lift, if they had the space.

Shortly before six a.m., Caitlin put her suitcases outside her hall door and took one last look at the beautiful seaside room which she had first entered so happily.

The bags were cumbersome, and in the darkness she stumbled on the walkway to the lobby in the main villa. She had not wanted to risk requesting the luggage be picked up for fear some slight noise might alert Jake. The possibility of a confrontation with him was something she wanted to avoid at all costs. Better for both of them that he discover she was gone when he woke later. Caitlin had no doubt he would be relieved that he was well rid of her. But her teaming up with the Carli siblings would have angered him. He didn't trust Nico.

At the desk she made sure that the bill was in order and picked up her passport. There were no phone calls or faxes charged to the suite. Strange. Jake must have paid for them at the time.

Little explanation was due the night desk clerk other than that her "business associate" Signore Riordan would be leaving somewhat later. And with her passport now safely in her purse, she settled down in a chair, half hidden by a huge potted palm to wait for the Carlis.

Her wait was short. Within 10 minutes Nico strode past her on his way to the desk. Quickly, she stood and called his name.

"Signorina, what are you doing out so early?" Nico's surprise was evident and not just by the sight of her."I thought you said you were planning on a leisurely departure?"

"Jake will be leaving later. I…that is, Francesca said the other day when I mentioned my next stop was Milan that I might catch a ride with you. I know she was just joking, but is there any possibility…?"

Nico's hand was warm on hers as he grasped the situation. "You and Signore Riordan are going in different directions?"

Caitlin nodded. It was the understatement of the year. "Of course, if you don't have room or have changed your plans…?"

"We would be delighted," Nico said quickly, his pleasure apparent. "Your luggage? Shall I get it for you?"

Caitlin pointed it out near the door. "I've checked out. Everything is taken care of."

"Then, I will be just a moment." Nico was suddenly boyish, his face animated. As if something had suddenly occurred to him, he turned back on his way to the desk. "Signor Riordan is aware of your change of plans?

Caitlin shook her head. "We…uh…settled last night on a change. He meant to drive me to Milan and we would part there. I'd rather ride with you, if you're sure it's all right."

Nico's face grew even brighter. "I'll only be a moment. I settled our bill last evening and have only to drop off the keys."

He was as good as his word, and shortly with Caitlin's luggage in hand, was leading the way to the car, a comfortable sedan. In the back, a blanket folded under her head, was a drowsy Francesca. Nico held the passenger door of the front seat open for Caitlin and she got in. Francesca roused enough to take in what was happening.

"Caitlin! You are coming with us?" A smile broke over her sleepy face. "Very good. But where is the handsome Jake?"

"Jake has business that will keep him here a while," Caitlin said stiffly. "Nico has come to my rescue. If you don't mind…"

"Why should I?" Francesca yawned and clapped her hand over her mouth. "I plan to sleep most of the time. You can keep Nico company." A thought popped into her head. "And Jake will meet you in Milan?"

Caitlin shook her head, not wanting to talk about Jake or think about him. "Some new development has come up. He has to attend to it."

"Too bad." Francesca yawned again. "Wake me up when you stop at one of the service areas. I could use some coffee." And with that she sank back onto her folded blanket and closed her eyes."

Nico finished stowing Caitlin's luggage in the spacious trunk and got behind the wheel saying happily, "I'm glad we brought our father's car. My own needed a tune-up. There would not have been room for you…" Nico turned to the back seat, looked at the form of his sleeping sister. "Of course we could always have tied Francesca to the top of the car. She wouldn't have known the difference." He smiled flashing very white teeth in the tanned face.

Caitlin returned the smile with difficulty. Nico was very nice, but compared to Jake he was a boy. Fearful that Jake might come running out even now and make a scene, she held her breath until Nico pulled out of the hotel parking lot and headed for the public road.

As they passed the main sign for the hotel, Caitlin's heart plummeted. The morning they had arrived, Jake, wearing the boots, had stopped and pulled out the Stetson and camera from the trunk of the Mercedes. A gardener, an old man in wide trousers and blue work shirt who was tending the flowers at the base of the sign had been happy to help. Jake showed him how to use the camera and the man had taken a picture of Jake and Caitlin. If only she had thought to hand him her camera, as well, she would have a picture of Jake. Memories would have to suffice.

Caitlin leaned against the headrest and closed her eyes. "You are tired. You couldn't have slept much last night," Nico said.

"No…I had things on my mind."

"It is none of my business but I gather your parting was not amicable?"

Hoping to put an end to the interrogation, Caitlin's answer was brief. "Jake and I both have commitments back home."

Her brusque tone worked. Nico was all apologies. "Forgive my intrusion." Then abruptly changing the subject he added, "Perhaps you would benefit from Francesca's example." He laughed. "It is a family joke that the minute she begins a long trip, she sleeps. Saves her energy for later."

Caitlin responded with a wan smile. She had done the same every time she had been in the car with Jake, or so it had seemed. Perhaps because she had trusted Jake, felt safe in his hands. How ironic, she thought.

Within minutes they were back on the Autostrada, retracing the route Caitlin and Jake had taken so blithely a few days before. But very quickly Nico exited for another highway taking them up over the mountains toward Milan.

Instead of bolstering Caitlin's spirits, the view of the Cote d'Azur from on high had the opposite effect. Every word they had exchanged, every comment of Jake's came back to haunt her.

To distract herself she made small talk with Nico. Both he and Francesca were at university, Nico not yet sure whether he wanted to follow his father into banking or venture into some other field. Their mother was an art historian who lectured around the country. Francesca had made noises about going into design.

Caitlin was given to understand in the kindest of terms that Francesca was something of a dilettante, who if she would only put her mind and energy to it, might make a name for herself in interiors or possibly fashion. Milan, after all, was the fashion capital of Italy, certainly on a par with Paris, and with any number of potential mentors.

The problem was, Nico said, Francesca could not decide which branch to devote her considerable talents to. "She has to do a little growing up," Nico said. A strange remark, Caitlin thought, from a younger brother.

"And you, Signorina, you mentioned being in business. What is your field?"

Caitlin told him briefly about the small shop in Hartford where she and her colleague Antonietta repaired heirloom clothing and other textiles. The fancy name for what she did was art conservator, she said, but for most of their clients, she was just the woman who could preserve something old they considered precious, something handed down through the generations and not always taken care of properly.

"But, then you, too, are an artisan. You and Francesca probably have much in common if you could get to her serious side." It was, Nico pointed out, nearing the end of the term and Francesca was weary of classes, weary of gloomy weather and of parental supervision.

"She wanted to go a livelier spot, for spring break, but Mama put her foot down and said also that I had to go, too." He smiled engagingly. "Not that it was hard to do. Sunshine has been in short supply this past winter in Milano."

Nico chatted on and Caitlin let him ramble, grateful that he did not mention Jake again nor question her about the fiancé she had mentioned.

Two hours into the trip, and now back in Italy, Nico pulled into a Motta Auto grill for gas. They woke Francesca who apparently slept through everything and went inside where they bought coffee, rolls and oranges from the small concession. Caitlin exclaimed over the freshness and texture of the rolls, but then as Jake had declared more than once, it was difficult to find bad food in Italy.

Would she never get her mind off Jake? She wondered what his reaction had been to wake and find her gone. Had he missed her at all, or had it been a case of "good riddance?" No doubt it was the latter. Caitlin had caused him enough trouble.

Returning to the car, Francesca decided she wanted to drive. Nico argued with her, but his sister persisted and Caitlin, looking at Nico, said, "Why don't I take the back seat for a while and you can play navigator for Francesca."

"It is not a navigator Francesca needs," said Nico grimly, "but a sense of fear. There are a lot of curves on the mountains ahead and she drives like a…a..cowboy."

It was the wrong simile, Caitlin thought, as she climbed into the car. Was there anything that didn't remind her of Jake?

Miraculously, Francesca decided to drive with caution and as they proceeded up through the mountain highway, Caitlin dozed off.

She slept as if she had been drugged, waking briefly, to see that Nico was once again behind the wheel. She woke later as the car stopped . They couldn't be in Milan this quickly.

"An accident, ahead, a bad one from the look of it," Francesca offered. Nico glanced over his shoulder to tell Caitlin, ""I'm going to walk up and see if I can get any information…"

He was back in a moment. "A bus and several cars involved. They're waiting for ambulances. Nobody dead, but several people are badly injured. We're in for a wait, I'm afraid."

"Damn," Francesca muttered. "I had plans for this afternoon."

Nico gave her a look. He turned to Caitlin, "The delay is a problem for you?"

She shook her head. "My room is reserved. They'll hold it."

"If they don't, you can stay with us. We've extra room," Francesca declared, her mood changing. She was, Caitlin decided, a little spoiled, but on the whole warm-hearted and likeable.

It was mid-afternoon by the time they pulled into Milan. The delay at the accident site had been a long one and then they had stopped for another brief meal at yet another roadside *tavola calda*. With nothing to do but dwell on the fact that had Jake been present, somehow things would be different, Caitlin put in a miserable few hours.

As the distance separating them widened, the knot in her chest grew larger. In spite of her best intentions, she kept hearing Jake's voice, seeing his face, remembering their various outings.

On the outskirts of the city, Caitlin asked that they drop her near a taxi stand so she could make her way to the hotel. Nico would not hear of it.

By the time they had located the clean, if dreary, Albergo Marche, it was growing late. Caitlin took one look at the exterior and her heart sunk further. Francesca made an unflattering noise and turned to Caitlin. "You can't stay there even if it's for only one night. Come home with us."

Caitlin demurred but Nico added his entreaties to his sister's. "I will take you to the train station tomorrow with no trouble. Say you will allow us to take you to our place."

"Your parents?"

"Are not expected back from Naples until tomorrow. Mama is lecturing at the Museo de Paoli and Papa went with her on a rare

vacation. Besides they enjoy the company of our friends…"
Francesca was at her most engaging.

Caitlin, disheartened by the exterior of the hotel, thought it no place to spend a lonely night in her present state of mind. "If you're sure…"

Nico's answer was to swing the car around in mid traffic. "But, my reservation," Caitlin protested.

"You can call them from our house…say you were delayed because of the accident and will forfeit the deposit," urged Francesca who had an answer for everything it seemed.

The Carli flat, located in an upscale neighborhood, was large and attractive. The spacious rooms were comfortable rather than plush, but the art adorning the walls and tables, most of it centuries old, was exceptional.

Caitlin's guess that the works were extremely valuable, if not priceless, was confirmed by Nico. "Most of these are my mother's inherited from her family. A few she has acquired over the years."

He stopped in front of a dark oval portrait of a child in princely velvets, the small round face haunting in its unhappiness. "This she found in an outbuilding of an estate used by her family as a summer place before World War II. Everything else was ruined. My mother thinks it may be worth more than anything here."

"Poor baby. He looks so sad."

"You think so?" Nico peered at the dark colors. I don't think anyone else has commented on that aspect."

Caitlin stared into the childish eyes, noting again the bleakness. Or was the misery she saw there a reflection of her own unhappy state?

The room she was shown to was commodious and welcoming, the furniture light and airy, and again she was grateful that the Carlis had prevailed upon her to spend the night. She had called the hotel to cancel her reservation as soon as they arrived. As she was unpacking her night things, she heard the phone ring.

For a second, the dream that Jake had tracked her down caused her heart to hammer. But, there was a knock on her door, and she realized she must reconcile herself to the fact that she'd never see him again. It was crazy to think he'd look for her.

Out in the *salotto*, she found Nico waiting for her to offer her a choice of beverages. "We'll eat a little later. The woman who cooks for us has left roast chicken and *insalata* plus a *minestra*, a kind of stew that Francesca loves." Nico laughed drily. "Francesca, unfortunately, has taken off. A friend called. She'll be back a little later. If you don't mind having only me for a dinner companion..."

Caitlin shook her head, took the chair that Nico indicated.. "Of course not. I doubt I'll be very good company..."

Nico sat down opposite her. "I think you have spent a very bad day." Caitlin shot him a look, but there was only kindness in his tone and nothing threatening about his presence.

"I'll be all right. Just a mild head ache," she lied.

It was well past midnight when she pleaded weariness having refused Nico's repeated invitations to try Milan's night life. He had drunk glass after glass of wine following the meal, at least two cocktails before eating, and his words had become slurred. Francesca had not returned, calling only to apologize to Caitlin which Nico had relayed, and saying she would be very late, that she was going to some club.

Nico had apologized earlier for his sister's bad manners, noting that Francesca was making the most of her parents' absence.

Throughout the evening Nico's behavior toward her had been exemplary. He showed an amazing knowledge of Renaissance art and admitted that had he not been expected as the only son to follow in his father's footsteps, he might have enjoyed a career in the field.

That, in turn, led to a discussion on the differences between European and American men, with Caitlin attempting to cut it short when the subject began to veer toward attitudes toward women.

Nico persisted, and eventually the conversation swung to Caitlin and her charms. She realized he was well on his way to being drunk as the slurring grew more pronounced, his admiration for Caitlin expressed in extravagant terms.

To turn him off, she began walking around the room picking up one small art object after another and asking about its history. Caitlin was examining a small vessel he said had been found in the ruins near Pompeii, a miniature amphora, when she realized he was much too close, that she could feel his highly aromatic and warm breath on her neck.

"Signorina! Caitlin!" Quickly, she moved as he attempted to pin her next to the wall. With the small relic in hand, she fled toward the room she had been allotted and shutting the door behind her gave thanks for the key she'd noticed earlier in the door.

"Caitlin, Signorina, *per favore*, please I simply want to talk."

She thought it better not to answer other than to say that she was tired and going to bed and eventually the knocking on the door and pleading stopped. "What had she gotten herself into?" Far better the dreary hotel than this kind of scene, but who knew Francesca would take off like that?

Happily there was a bathroom off the bedroom and she quickly readied for bed and started pulling out her night things when there was more commotion in the hallway, giving way to loud exclamations in Italian, both a male and female voice, and eventually knocking on her door.

"Signorina. Will you please step out here?" It was not a voice she recognized but clearly one of authority. A female voice. that grew increasingly loud and agitated.

With trepidation Caitlin opened the door. A very large imposing woman stood there, fire in her eyes. A spate of Italian that came too fast for her to understand, then slowly it dawned on her as the woman began shaking a finger at her, the words were more like invectives.

The woman was Nico's mother and she was accusing Caitlin of seduction! Preying on her young son! Panicky, Caitlin looked for Nico to contradict her , but he was nowhere in sight. Nor was the father.

Caitlin attempted to explain, saying that Francesca and Nico had invited her to spend the night before taking the train to Lake Como. At that point Signora Carli caught sight of something in the room. She gave a loud scream and barreled past Caitlin to pounce on the small Pompeian artifact. Grabbing it, she came back to confront Caitlin and demonstrated her excellent command of the English language. "Thief. Thief," brandishing the object.

Caitlin found her tongue."I was looking at it when your son chased me in here."

"Lies," came the bombastic retort. "All lies." She marched into Caitlin's room and began pulling things out of her suitcase, obviously in search of other stolen goods. Signora Carli spotted Caitlin's handbag on the bureau and dumped it upside down.

Ashen-faced, Caitlin was speechless. Nothing she had remotely feared for a trip alone had prepared her for this eventuality. Just then help came from an unexpected quarter. Francesca was calling from the front entrance. She walked in, no evidence of heavy imbibing, to confront her mother.—first in Italian, then in English, ostensibly for Caitlin's benefit.

"Mama! What are you doing? Caitlin is a friend. We met her in Nice and asked her to stay the night."

There was another torrent from the matriarch as Caitlin began to stuff clothes back into the suitcase and purse. Still ashen-faced, she turned to Francesca. "Your mother thinks I was trying to seduce your brother and steal the small relic." She pointed to the vessel. "I was admiring it when he started chasing me. I fled to the bedroom and locked the door with it in my hand."

Caitlin was gratified to see Francesca also speechless and continued, " I'll go now. Where can I find a taxi?"

"You can't go now. Where will you go? It's after 1 a.m. Your train doesn't leave until 8 a.m. Mama has to know you are telling the truth about Nico. It's not the first time he's become amorous after drinking too much."

"I will sit in the train station," Caitlin said, trying to steady her shaking legs. "Please tell me how to get a taxi."

"No, you can't leave. It's not safe."

"Then I'll walk," and resolutely Caitlin moved past Francesca and her mother to the main hall.

It had ended with Francesca pleading with her father to take over. He had come from his study where he had been on the phone. "A matter of some gravity," he told Caitlin, referring to the call. "Please, Signorina won't you stay the night? I will calm Mama. She is prone to overprotecting her son."

"Grazie, no," she told Signore Carli. "I'm afraid that is impossible now. I must get to the train station. Please tell me how I can get a taxi."

After a certain amount of half-hearted argument, he placed a telephone call. He seemed distracted, his mind far away. At last he said, "There will be a taxi at the front door of the apartment building in 10 minutes."

"Thank you," she said and pulled open the large front door, Francesca's entreaties still in her ears, and escaped to the open, waiting elevator, pushing the down button.

The taxi took far longer to arrive and the ride to the train station a circuitous one. By the time she arrived, it was nearly 3 a.m. At the train station, a stark, cavernous structure, she realized she had nearly five hours to wait before she could board. There were a few unsavory characters around, but happily most of them were asleep. The waiting room was closed, she was told by a night watchman, for security reasons. He offered her a seat in a small office, if she cared to do so. She accepted.

Sagging into a chair, she gasped aloud, "Oh, God, how could I ever have been so stupid?" She berated herself at length, sank back in the chair, afraid to close her eyes.

She was able to board the train for Como at 7:30 and after purchasing her ticket and wrestling her luggage into the car found her seat.

Caitlin acknowledged she was exhausted but couldn't allow herself to relax until she was at the hotel in Cernobbio, not far from Como, and on the lake. If only....

She had tried to squelch the thoughts through the long night but try as she might, she couldn't help but think that she had brought all this on herself. Had she not blown up at Jake, she might be traveling with him still, in comfort and, yes, protected from her own foolishness.

Taking off with the Carlis had been the first mistake. Staying at their apartment had been the second and then running abruptly out of their home, had been the third. Thank God, she had made it through the night safely and was now on the train.

But the relief was short-lived as she began thinking of Jake. It didn't help telling herself how irrational she was being, that she had known the man for only a few days. Feelings and logic often took divergent roads. The last week had taught her that.

Chapter 8

An hour later, oblivious to the pastoral scenes the train windows framed, she arrived in Como. The small, neat train station, on a narrow grade was shrouded in mist as was the resort itself.

Caitlin collected her luggage and stood alone, shivering on the platform. A fine rain began to fall, and she clutched her thin jacket around her, her already low spirits plummeting further. Wearily, she swept back wet tendrils of hair from her face.

Memory of the warmth and sunshine she had left the day before taunted her. She must put Jake and the Riviera behind her. The enormity of her loss struck with new force.

Jake, Jake. Her heart was a lump within her chest. Angry with herself for giving in to her emotions, she drew herself upright. She couldn't just stand there. Where were the porters?

To her right were stairs leading to the town's main piazza and waterfront. Could she manage to get her luggage down by herself. Fiercely she swiped at her face as unshed tears blinded her.

She turned, took a step and collided with an immovable force. Caitlin gasped with fright as strong arms gripped her with a hard urgency, then pressed her to his damp, looming bulk.

Incredulous, she heard the familiar voice. "Cait, Cait, you little fool."

Unbelieving still, she managed to free herself enough to let her eyes and mind absorb what her body already knew.

"Oh, Jake," she whispered into his coat as he gathered her roughly back to him. "It's been so awful. Is it really you?" The tears she had held back came now in a silent, unchecked rush.

Jake held her from him, just enough so he could look down into her swollen eyes. "You'll wish it weren't when I get through with you," he muttered. "My God, do you know how long I've been searching for you?"

And taking out a clean, white handkerchief, he began to mop her wet face, pausing once, with a muffled sound to gently trace her trembling mouth with an index finger.

.Jake's touch was enough to start Caitlin shivering violently. "Come on," he said brusquely, "let's get you out of the rain." He picked up one of her suitcases with his left hand and flexed his right before picking up the other. Seeing her look of concern, he explained, "An old break. Acts up in damp weather."

She reached out to take her suitcase from him. "Let me carry it."

Jake's smile was mocking, warming her blood. He started walking. Caitlin followed, unable to take her gaze from his face, wanting to take his hurting hand in hers and comfort him.

"How did you break it?"

"We were playing touch football and both of them landed on top of me."

"Touch football?" She grinned. "Sounds more like the knock-down, drag-out variety to me. Who's both?"

"College suitemates. Paolo Cimino and Dan—ford Jones…"

Caitlin's eyebrows rose. "Danford Jones? For a second she had thought he was going to say Daniel. Not that it would have meant anything. Daniel was one of the most common names for males.

Jake's gaze was on the steps, a short distance away. " Danford, the Third, no less. Mayflower roots. Very upper crust." Then loudly, "Here we go. Watch your step. The car's not far away."

Caitlin followed him. There was so much she didn't know about Jake, she realized. Where he'd gone to college, who his friends were. She was, well, greedy to know everything about him. At some point she would ask him.

Within minutes they were inside the Mercedes, Caitlin's luggage stowed in the trunk next to Jake's. He sat behind the wheel, making no attempt to set the car in motion. With the rain still falling, it was as if they were in a cocoon, just the two of them. She thought of last night, the long hours in the train station, unable to believe that the nightmare was over. That Jake, her shield, was close enough to touch.

He stared at her, then reached over and with the back of one finger, gently wiped one remaining drop of moisture from her cheek. "You've a lot of explaining to do, Caitlin Harris," he said at last. "Where on earth have you been the last 30 hours? I called the hotel in Milan. They said you'd cancelled." He closed his eyes and opened them. "Talk about going crazy."

She stared up at him from under the sooty lashes, made dark by the moisture. Why would Jake care so much about her well being? It was almost as if he had designated himself her protector. A tantalizing thought flashed into her head. Could it mean that Jenny no longer held first place in Jake's affections…No, no! It was crazy to think that way.

"I caught a ride with the Carlis. There was a bad accident on the way. We got held up." She paused, took a long breath. "When we got to the hotel it was so awful, Jake, compared to the one in Nice, and I was so..so.." She didn't finish the sentence but her tone made it clear that she had been miserable.

"And?"

"Francesca invited me to spend the night with their family. They had a guest room."

"I guessed as much. The concierge in Nice refused to give out their address. I tried to find their phone number. No luck."

"I'm sorry you were upset." Truth was, she wasn't. He'd been worried about her….

He gave her a long look, unsettling in its intensity. "You and I are going to have a talk—later. Now let's get to the hotel, see what your next accommodations look like and get into some dry clothes."

The Villa Regina was on the west coast of Lago di Como in the small town of Cernobbio, a few miles north of the city of Como. Miraculously the reserved rooms were ready for occupancy.

The third floor suite featured a sitting room with pull-out couch, a bedroom with bath and a balcony. A small, flowering seaside park tended by a gardener separated them from the lake which was surrounded by mountains. Jake's first move was to pull open the curtains and step out through the French doors.   He called to her. "The mist is rising. You can see the water."

Caitlin was inspecting the suite. A huge, painted Venetian bedstead in cream, aquamarine and gold was the focal point. The bed, a matching chest of drawers, along with gold velvet draperies and paneled shutters set the elegant tone of the bedroom.

The sitting room was smaller with a commodious cushy sofa, a couple of easy chairs and desk, and half hidden in one corner, a small refrigerator stocked with soft drinks and miniature wines and brandies.

She heard Jake call and moved to the balcony to stand next to him. She breathed in deeply, happiness suffusing her body. She had thought nothing could be more beautiful than Portofino, but this matched it easily. Formed by glaciers and surrounded by mountains, the jewel-like lake stretched before them. Large drooping pines and flowering bushes outlined the park below. Across the lake the mountain was still shrouded in mist.

As she stood entranced gazing at the scene before her, Jake at her side, the sun broke through. "Oh, look, Jake!" It was like an omen.

"Should burn off the fog in no time," he answered her, his eyes on her rather than the scenery. "We'll be able to see across to the opposite side shortly."

He turned back to the bedroom, gazed at the huge bed and then through the open double doors to the sitting room beyond.

Caitlin caught his eye and her face warmed. "The sofa won't be that comfortable. I'll take it."

"You'll sleep in the bed. It's your room." Jake's tone brooked no argument. "Knowing you're safe and sound, I'll sleep like a log tonight." Stretching out on the sofa and pronouncing it more than comfortable, he announced, "I'm hungry. How about you? "

At some point she would tell him about the horrible evening she had spent including sitting up all night in the train station. But she'd had no breakfast and suddenly she had an appetite. "Where should we go?"

"We can try the dining room downstairs. I caught a glimpse on the way to the elevators. Afterward we can explore the park. It's getting more pleasant by the minute."

Caitlin watched as he retrieved his suitcase from the bedroom where the bellboy had stowed all three. Jake had been worried about her she could tell. But had it been because he felt something for her or simply fearful because he thought her too unsophisticated to be on her own? Well, she'd proved him right.

She stopped him as he was going back to the sitting room with the suitcase. "The dresser has enough drawers for both of us."

He turned and rested the bag on top of the ornate chest of drawers with crystal pulls, then teased, "You won't feel compromised, having our clothes on such intimate terms?"

Her face grew warm. She met his gaze and said "I had a lot of time to think last night. For what it's worth, I realize now that you are …trustworthy. I should not have let Claude, or Nico, get to me."

"Claude meant no harm. I suspect he thought he was merely setting a spark to tinder. Though last night I could have wrung his neck. *And Nico Carli's,* " he muttered.

Caitlin suddenly decided he didn't have to know about all what had happened last night. There would be fireworks.

Suddenly it dawned on her that she didn't know where he had spent last night and asked him.

He shot her a disgusted look. "Guess."

"Not the Albergo Marchi?"

"None other. They just happened to have a cancelled reservation," he added drily.

"Was it awful?"

"Yes, but not for the reasons you think. I kept imagining you with that Romeo…"

Caitlin was silent. No need to get Jake upset. But her expression must have given her away..

He was staring at her, his mouth set in a thin line. "Something happened didn't it?"

Again she didn't answer. "It did, didn't it?" His voice grew steely. "What happened? I presume it was at their home. Where were their parents?"

"Not yet back from a lecture tour."

"And that flirt sister of his? Don't tell me she was content to spend a quiet evening at home."

"Francesca went out and …. "Caitlin paused trying to think the best way to tell Jake about her untoward evening.. "Nico was fine at first, telling me all about his family's art collection. But he kept drinking—a whole bottle of wine…He…he…started to…."

Jake looked murderous and so she quickly resumed. " But nothing happened. I went into the bedroom and locked the door."

Apparently she was not convincing. "And then what happened?" Jake demanded.

"The parents came home and…and…"

"And what?"

"The mother accused me of …of seducing her son …" She gave a ironic laugh, "and…"

"My God! What else?"

"Of trying to steal a small, very rare piece of pottery dating back to Pompeii?" Caitlin's voice was shaking now as she remembered the scene. "I was holding it, admiring it when he…he…made a move …" She paused in the face of his grim silence. "And that's when I locked myself in the bedroom."

"And what happened?"

"I left."

"You left?" He was incredulous. "And where did you go?"

"To the train station?"

"What! What time?"

"About 3 a.m. I sat there and waited for the first train to Como."

"You sat in that monstrous train station by yourself in the middle of the night? Where anyone could have accosted you? And they let you go!" Jake' expression was that of a mad man. "I'll kill him. So help me, if I ever see him again, I will. "And you…" he rounded on her. "You deserve a thrashing …"

Suddenly she was very tired. "It's over." She tried a different tack. "I'm hungry and I'm tired. I'd like to take a nap…." Caitlin stared at the bed longingly.

Jake stared at her. "You didn't sleep at all last night?"

She shook her head. He made a sound that was not pleasant and moved to the phone. English was understood by Room Service as well and she heard him ask for, coffee, hot chocolate and rolls.

He hung up. "Get into bed and I'll bring in the food when it comes," he ordered and with that he moved to the outer room and closed the door behind him. For once she did as she was told, too tired to protest that she didn't want to be bossed, that he had no right to treat her as if he were her guardian and not just some traveler she picked up along the way. It didn't sound too classy, but it was the truth, she reminded herself.

The room service was not speedy, but Caitlin was all nerves and couldn't fall asleep. She'd taken off her outer clothes and put on a robe, then flipping the spread back, lay on top of the blankets.

When Jake knocked on the door and appeared with a tray of rolls, butter and pots of hot chocolate, coffee and steaming milk she had calmed down.

She took a roll and spread it liberally with butter. "Thank you, I was hungry." She wolfed it down. The hot chocolate, in part because it was poured from a silver pot, was delicious, and she sipped it greedily..

Jake had coffee and one of the rolls, sitting across from her and using a small desk as a table. "What are you going to do while I nap?" she wanted to know.

"I'm not sure I can leave you alone. You're a baby when it comes to taking care of yourself."

She sat up, indignant. "Stop making me out to be hopelessly naïve. I can take care of myself."

"Sure you can," he said the sarcasm rolling off his tongue. "Not with a thousand Romeos afoot. Didn't you notice? The lobby downstairs is crawling with them. "I'm not letting you out of my sight." Now it was her turn to stare at him. If she didn't know better, she'd think Jake was on a mission to look after her.

Caitlin made a face and received a warning look in return. Too tired to put up a fight, she turned her face into the pillow and drifted off at once. She slept several hours and when she awoke, refreshed, she heard Jake in the outer room. Hastily, she gathered clothing and went into the bathroom.

When she called to him a short while later, he opened the door, saw she was dressed, and gave her an approving glance. "Ready to explore? It's too beautiful to stay inside any longer."

"I can hardly wait to look around."

They checked out the hotel's glassed-in dining room overlooking the lake but both were eager to get outside and decided it would be worth their while to explore other possibilities for lunch. The sun as Jake had predicted had burnt off the mist and the blue waters of Como were dotted with white sails. The mountain rising emerald green and majestic on the opposite side of the lake was now completely visible.

Caitlin breathed in a sigh of happiness. "The poet Virgil," she said, quoting from a guide book she'd devoured earlier, "called Como the greatest lake. I can see why." She took in the centuries-old villas and their gardens ringing the water, the snow-capped Alps in the distance, the graceful, drooping pines and flowered terraces that framed the lake.

"And what do you call it?" asked Jake, clearly amused by her enthusiasm.

"The most romantic place I've ever seen. I'm so glad I insisted with the travel agent," she began, then stopped herself, all too mindful that she was here on a solitary honeymoon trip with a man she had known for only a few days. Quickly, she changed the subject. "Where shall we go? Explore Como? Or, I should have asked, perhaps you have some business errand?"

He shook his head to the last question. Jake's stated purpose when he proposed they travel together was to look at small hotels. As far as Caitlin could tell he didn't seem all that concerned about his original plans. Now he steered her in the direction of the garden.

As they strolled through the small flowering park, Caitlin studied the mountain looming large across the lake. She couldn't see any roads amidst the dense foliage and wondered aloud if there were other dwellings on the slopes, perhaps smaller than the grand villas at the water's edge.

"You'll be able to tell tonight when the lights come on," Jake assured her as they made their way toward a small coffee bar at the end of the park on a point jutting out into the water. "Cappuccino?"

Caitlin nodded. The prospect of sitting at one of the small tables on the pier sounded idyllic.

"This must be the most beautiful of all the Italian lakes," she murmured as a few minutes later they nursed the delicious frothy blend, a beverage which Caitlin thought must be second only to wine in national popularity.

Jake laughed. "You have no point of comparison. Wait until you see Maggiore and then decide."

She nodded. Stresa on Lake Maggiore would be her last and longest stop, her hotel, according to the travel agent, a few doors from the Grand Hotel where Hemingway had stayed. She turned abruptly back from the water to find Jake studying her. His expression caused the inner turmoil to start.

He had wanted to talk, he'd said, when they got into the car at the train station that morning. She wanted it, too. At least she thought she did. She was torn between clearing the air and wanting them to go on just as they were now.

All he'd talked about thus far was Nico—and Caitlin's abrupt leave taking. So far Jake had said nothing about Jenny, had refrained from mentioning Daniel. Nothing had changed between them after the separation, Caitlin reminded herself. ... But something was different.   If only she could figure out what. There was an intensity about Jake now that had not been there before.

When he suggested a drive along the lake, she agreed readily. They drove north along the west bank, a steep mountain on their left, to Cadenabia where Jake pointed out the ferry could take them and the car across the lake to Bellagio, the famous resort.

Lake Como, she'd seen from the map, formed an inverted Y with Bellagio in the center, the two arms at the southern end. "Of course we could also go back down to Como and drive up the other shore to Bellagio and then take the ferry back to Cadenabia."

"Oh, yes, sounds wonderful," Caitlin enthused.

"Let's plan on it tomorrow when we can get an earlier start. Perhaps dinner tonight in Como?"

Again, she agreed. Suddenly she was hungry. As they continued to drive north, stopping now and then to get out and admire a compelling view of the lake, they came to a small roadside *alimentari*, comprising a store and deli. "Shall we go in and see if they can put together a couple of sandwiches? We can stop at one of the overlooks and have lunch," Jake suggested.

"Oh, let's," she said enthusiastically, remembering the casual meal they'd had in Monaco. Inside the small market, Jake took over with her consent. Crusty hollow rolls split and filled with turkey and ham, a small container of cured dark olives, a thin wedge of sublime fontinella cheese, fresh pears imported from who knew where, paper cups and a bottle of local white wine.

"It's not a picnic, it's a feast," Caitlin said as they settled themselves in the Mercedes, the top down to take advantage of the weather which had turned from the morning's rain and mist to a glorious blue sky reflected in the water.

Jake drove to a small parking area next to the water and they tore into the sandwiches, fresh air fueling their hunger. On either side of them were small villas with boxes of red and pink geraniums and cheery petunias at every window, ornate urns filled with showy blooms decorating the terraces. When they had consumed the lot, they drove slowly back down the curving roadway.

As they neared their hotel, Jake pointed out an imposing structure, Villa d'Este. "Very grand," Caitlin noted. "And very old?"

"Dates to the Sixteenth Century. Perhaps the most elegant hotel in Europe, right at the top anyway."

"Too elegant, perhaps," said Caitlin.

"Umm, but not for the right occasion."

She looked at him, looked quickly away. Honeymoon with Jenny was obviously what he had in mind.

She thought of the kiss they had shared that first night in Nice. It had been a matter of good wine, magical moonlight and proximity. Nothing more. That it hadn't meant anything to Jake was all too clear. He'd been anything but romantic. And in most of their encounters, they usually ended up sparring.

At the train station this morning he had been caring and concerned. But then he'd changed to being sardonic and brusque. He seemed to flip flop between the two attitudes, she thought.

Caitlin looked over at him and saw Jake stifle a yawn. "You didn't get enough sleep last night either?"

He shook his head. "Let's take a quick look around Como and then head back to the rooms to relax before dinner. They passed their hotel in Cernobbio and were soon back in Como. On the main street he pointed out a two-story Standa, a *pasticerria*, another *alimentari.*

"There's a *super mercato* two blocks over I spotted this morning, looking for gas before the train came," Jake said. "Standa's on a par with our discount stores, but the merchandise is a bit different, could be interesting."

"Great. I need a few incidentals." Jake parked the car and they sauntered in, Caitlin all eyes for the bins and shelves of merchandise. She quickly discovered that the best items were not textiles which she was given to understand were found in specialty shops. But the kitchenware was a different matter. The Italians were masters of combining style and functionality.

Jake who had wandered into the extensive wine section now came back with a bottle of Pinot Grigio and watched with amusement as Caitlin chose a half dozen melamine trays, sleek, colorful with engaging scenes.

"My parents and Gran eat their evening meals in front of the television watching the news," she explained. "Extras for friends. They'll fit neatly in the bottom of the suitcase."

"And nothing for Caitlin?"

"Como was once the center of the silk industry, but I'm not sure that any of the merchandise ends up here. A scarf or two for family gifts would be nice."

"We'll inquire at the desk back at the hotel," Jake promised. "But you're right, more likely the place to shop for such things is Milan." At the mention of the nearby city, she wrinkled her nose and changed the subject. She'd had enough of Milan for this trip although had she been with Jake she was certain it would have been wonderful. Paying for their purchases they returned to the car and were soon back at the hotel.

Upstairs, Caitlin faced up to an awkward situation. That morning she had been too tired to care, but now she realized privacy for both of them was a matter of planning. There were massive double doors between the sitting room and the bedroom. The bathroom, furthermore, was off the bedroom, as was the balcony and view. If she shut the door while she napped, Jake was cut off from both.

"I'll the leave the door open," she murmured. "In case you feel like sitting on the balcony."

Jake was matter of fact about the situation. "Not necessary. I'll probably doze off in a minute." But having made the offer, Caitlin was uneasy about rescinding it.

Seeing that Jake had found a pillow and extra blankets in a closet, she took off her shoes and curled up on the bed, accepting one of the blankets he tossed to her. Air off the lake, while not cold, was not exactly balmy either now in the late afternoon.

A slight noise made her turn toward the sitting room. Jake had shut one of the double doors, left the other slightly ajar affording her a measure of privacy. She smiled, secure in the knowledge that he was in the next room, a mere few feet away, and feeling safe, fell asleep.

It was dusk when she awoke. She heard a key in the outer hall door and realized that Jake had been out. In a moment he peered around the open door, a couple of small bags in his arms. "Sleeping beauty is awake at last. You certainly are a sound napper."

She roused, ran her fingers through her hair, the experience of having a man in her bedroom a new one. Trying to look at ease despite her grogginess she propped the pillows behind her and sat up, "You're not going to try to tell me I was snoring, I hope."

Jake grinned. "No, but I thought you'd have heard me out on the balcony earlier. You never moved."

That he had watched her while she slept was unnerving. Not meeting his gaze, she glanced at the bags. "Where have you been?"

"I found another small *alimentari*. More cheese to go with your wine, if you like."

It was impossible, but she was hungry again. "Yes, to both."

He unwrapped the packages. "We've some ementhaler—what we call Swiss cheese back home plus a handy gadget with corkscrew and knife to open the wine I bought earlier, glasses from the frigo bar in the sitting room and paper plates. Oh, yes, and aqua minerale to add to your wine, if you choose."

"It sounds like a party."

"It is. On the balcony. I didn't think we'd be able to improve on the view so we'll have our pre-prandial here and then a late supper, if you agree."

"Sounds marvelous."

Jake moved to the open French doors and beckoned to Caitlin. "You were wondering if anyone lived on the opposite mountain. Come look."

She pushed aside the blanket, swung her legs over the side of the bed and went to stand next to him, very conscious of his height without her shoes on.

"How beautiful!" In the settling dusk, the lights of the homes on the distant mountain had come on, the effect like so many twinkling fairy lamps.

Jake began arranging his purchases on the small balcony table. "It's not exactly hot out here. You might want a sweater."

Caitlin nodded. The lake air was clean and fresh and invigorating. She went to get a wrap.

They sat for nearly an hour, basking in the beauty of the evening, drinking and eating sparsely. Caitlin left the balcony reluctantly to head for the shower. She gathered underclothing from the suitcases, vowing to unpack later, and moved to the bathroom.

She came out clad in her robe to find Jake gone, both doors to the sitting room closed. She tapped and when he answered told him the bathroom was free.

She busied herself at the bureau, realizing getting dressed would be awkward unless she hurried while he was still in the shower. Next time she'd take her outer clothes into the bathroom as well.

As soon as the bathroom door closed behind Jake she threw off her kimono and quickly got into a skirt and top.

She had just started to dry her hair when Jake came out in slacks, his feet and chest bare. Her gaze fastened on the dark, damp curls of his head, the darker ones on his chest and quickly looked away. She swallowed, her throat dry. But in a minute he was gone, the doors to the sitting room once again closed.

When he tapped on the connecting door 10 minutes later, she was ready. They drove into Como again, this time to the street that fronted on the southern end of the lake.

"Something light or full meal?" Jake asked as he parked the car, and they set out to explore the various shops and eating places.

"Definitely light. I feel as if I've been eating all day."

Jake grinned. "Goes with the territory. Don't worry we'll walk our late supper off."

Flowering cherry trees lined the street opposite the water creating a wonderland of delicate color and scent. After exploring briefly they came to a small tavola calda at a corner and going inside agreed to the young proprietor's suggestion.

Tosti was an ambrosial delight of mozzarella and ham on thick homemade bread grilled on a special iron. Combined with a green salad and followed by *macedonia* which turned out to be a fresh fruit cup, it was, again, the perfect meal.

Afterward they retraced their steps, enjoying the reflection of colorful Japanese lanterns outlining a small marina on the water.

"How beautiful!" Caitlin drank in the scene. The breeze had shaken the cherry blossoms from the trees, filling the sidewalks with the rose-colored petals. As they walked, the crush of blooms under their feet sent up a fragrant scent adding to the already impossibly romantic setting.

Oh, Daniel, you don't know what you're missing, she thought. But then she had doubts he'd even notice, his mind back home on the business.

In Piazza Cavour, a group of young musicians were performing a medley of rock ballads in the square. Caitlin exclaimed over the choice of music.

Jake was matter of fact about it. " Kids are kids wherever you are. Music is the universal language and even in Italy, Verdi has his rivals."

They had no sooner sat down on the cool, wide steps of a building , then more people came and Caitlin, moving to make room for them, found herself very close to Jake. The fear that he would think she was seeking intimacy never got a chance to form. Jake threw an arm around her shoulders.

All around them young lovers were in similar embrace. "We don't want to look out of place," Jake said gravely, as Caitlin's pulses raced.

The music poured over them as the youngsters moved smoothly from one rock ballad to another. A youth who had doing the vocals, began a Rod Stewart number. His liquid voice could not quite approximate the famous rasp, his accent disguising some of the words. Caitlin, in an effort to appear unaffected by Jake's proximity, sang along.

Jake looked down at her, amused. "Don't tell me you're a Rod Stewart fan."

"Definitely."

The music went on, the scent of cherry blossoms still in the air, a sweet haze enfolding them, Caitlin could feel herself melting into Jake, could feel him tense. But all he said was, "I never would have guessed. Who else do you like?"

She rattled off a list of groups ending with "Meatloaf."

"Meatloaf!!"

"I like raspy voices."

Jake squeezed her shoulders, laughing. "I'll have to practice."

The next selection was a love song. All around them the young lovers were kissing. "Let's get out of here," Jake growled abruptly and taking her hand pulled her to her feet, down the steps and out of the piazza. Without a word, her hand firmly gripped in his, he moved quickly toward the car.

The streets were more crowded than they had been earlier. At the car, Jake unlocked her door and put her inside. She watched as he came around to the driver's side, trying to read his expression in the dim light from adjacent stores.

He drove toward a small parking area near the water they had spotted earlier. Only one other car had parked there, some distance from them.

Caitlin watched the distant lanterns swaying in the breeze, the reflected colors swirling on the dark water. Scudding clouds obscured the nearly full moon for a few moments. Jake was silent.

Another love song, this one liquid and haunting, drifted down from the piazza. Jake swore and in the moonlight which suddenly flooded the car, she saw him run his hands through his hair.

Without warning his arms came around her, pulling her to him, his mouth finding hers in one long terrible, wonderful moment telling her everything she wanted to know. Jake wanted her as much as she wanted him. The knowledge loosened the flood gates. She kissed him back as he was kissing her, without restraint.

"Oh, Jake," she whispered.

He let her go abruptly, taking her arms which had crept around his neck and putting them in her lap. With a brutal twist of the key and a screech of brakes, he backed the car out of the parking spot and headed for the main street and the road to Cernobbio.

Devastated by the kiss as well as its abrupt conclusion, she hardly dare breathe on the way back to the hotel, much less steal a glance at Jake. Parking the car in the tight lot, Jake got out and took her to the door of the lobby. "Go to bed," he said.

"What?"

"Go to bed!" His voice was hoarse to the point of harshness.

"But what are you going to do?'

"Walk around the lake!"

"You can't! It must be hundreds of miles.".

"Good," he retorted. "Maybe by the time I've gone around it, I'll have regained my sanity."

*   *   *

Earlier in the day as Caitlin slept Jake had sent a fax to Paolo informing him the crisis was over. Now he made for the office again. The concierge of the Villa Regina was as obliging as he had been earlier. Signore Riordan was not to worry about the late hour. It was what the concierge was there for—to render assistance to the hotel's guests. And motioning Jake to come behind the desk to the inner office, the concierge, a balding, sad-eyed man with a tiny mustache, pointed out the phone, and then closed the door, leaving Jake alone.

The call to Paolo went through quickly, unlike the one he'd made the night before from his room in the Albergo Marchi. "You got my fax?" he asked. "Good. The danger is over, but there's-um-a complicating factor. No, I can't go into it right now. I'll work it out somehow. I have to."

Chapter 9

Caitlin entered the breakfast room the next morning determined not to let her anxiety show over last night's scene. Jake had left her a note in the suite's sitting room, the brief scrawl saying he would meet her downstairs. Finding the note instead of Jake did nothing for her already unnerved state.

She had not heard him come in the night before, nor heard him leave this morning She was not sure he had slept there at all, the pullout sofa tucked neatly away. Downstairs she asked the waiter to seat her at a table next to one of the large windows, although there was little to be seen on mist-shrouded Como this time of day.

Caitlin sipped the coffee she was served and was about to try one of the still warm sweet rolls when she saw Jake coming toward her. With studied nonchalance, she broke off a piece of the roll and put it into her mouth, rendering herself incapable of responding with more than a nod to his crisp, "Good morning."

She swallowed, nearly choking in her haste, as Jake seated himself. He reached for the silver pot and poured more coffee for her and then filled his own cup, his eyebrows lifting as she continued coughing.

"All right?" His voice was cool, impersonal, as different as possible from the feverish muttering of the night before.

She nodded, her heart plummeting. It was as she had feared. Jake regretted this second kiss—even more than he had the first in the moonlight in Nice. It had been the act of a man giving way to the music, the setting, the proximity of a member of the opposite sex. She knew she wasn't unattractive. Hadn't he told her so?

Caitlin had gone to bed to dream of Jake, her hopes high that he would tell her this morning that he loved her, not Jenny, and that she should forsake Daniel for him. The empty suite had been the first indication that all was not well. No, not true. The first indication was his behavior right after he kissed her when he pulled away from her. This morning his manner and tone of voice confirmed what she feared most. Last night meant nothing to him.

How stupid she had been. Whatever had made Jake act as he had the previous evening could be attributed to momentary madness. Caitlin stole a glance as he buried himself in the Tribune, taking a sip of coffee now and then. She might have been a statue for all the attention he was paying to her.

She forced herself to make conversation because to go on as they were was awkward. "You haven't eaten either? When I didn't see you, I assumed you had finished." She congratulated herself. Her tone was as impersonal as his had been.

He shook his head without looking at her. "I decided to attend to business first. I called home last night and my brother Harry told me there's an inn outside Lugano I might want to take a look at."

"Lugano?"

"Switzerland. Just across the border."

She put her cup back in its saucer with rather more force than was necessary causing a clatter. "You called after you dropped me off?"

"Somewhat later." His voice was testy as he continued. " "There's a six-hour time difference between here and home, remember? I wanted to wait until Harry was through work and say hello to everybody. Might as well have saved my breath."

Caitlin felt her cheeks grow warm. Jake had answered her in a tone that indicated it was none of her business whom he called or when. She pretended not to notice. "Nobody home?"

"Just Harry. Dad was at one of his club meetings. Mom and Jenny were out shopping."

Caitlin's heart sank further. Without a mother of her own, Jenny would depend on Jake's mother for advice. Clothes for her trousseau, furnishings for the new home... With unsteady hand, she reached for her coffee and nearly knocked the cup off its saucer.

"Caitlin!" Jake's gaze searched her face. Was her emotional state so apparent?

Quickly she fabricated an excuse. "Terrible headache this morning. I took a couple of tablets. Should start to work soon."

"Caitlin!" Jake's voice was urgent. "There are some things we have to talk about...some things you should know."

She lifted her face to look at him, met the dark blue gaze. It was too painful and she glanced away. He had said that before— when he had found her at the train station in Como. But they hadn't talked—not about anything but very superficial matters.

"About last night," he began in a dry tone. "It shouldn't have happened. I apologize—again." His voice was strained—as if he had betrayed his best friend. "You belong to Daniel, and it was wrong of me to take advantage of you...I've been wanting to tell you..."

"And, you have Jenny to think of," Caitlin interrupted looking at him at last, praying for him to contradict her.

There was a long silence. "Yes," Jake said, his voice coming to her as if from a long distance. "There's Jenny."

Caitlin felt the blood drain from her face, the knot in her chest a tangible thing. His kiss last night had said so many things or so she had interpreted it.

Nobody to blame but herself. She had gone into this traveling arrangement with her eyes wide open. On their very first day together Jake had told her about Jenny. Stupid, stupid she berated herself again.

She looked up at him, saw something in his eyes she couldn't fathom. She prayed it was not pity. It was the last thing she wanted from him.

Jake must not guess that she was devastated. Caitlin reached for the coffee pot, this time refilled both cups with a steady hand and summoning all her willpower looked directly at him.

"Look, it's not the end of the world. What happened last night was simply a matter of proximity—and an impossibly romantic setting." She tried to laugh, miraculously succeeded.

"You've the better part of a week left," Jake said, "before you go back to Daniel."

"Yes," she fibbed and wisecracked, "Let's hope the next time I say 'Jump,' he asks 'How high?'"

Jake's expression was fierce. That's what you hoped to accomplish with this trip, right?"

"One of the goals," she fibbed again. "I also proved I can manage on my own," she said, remembering almost at once how bereft and lonely she had felt before Jake had found her at the Como train station. He shot her a sardonic look.

Caitlin ignored it. "The hotel in Lugano. Are you going to see it today?"

"Why do you want to know?"

"I always wanted to visit Switzerland. Unless I'll be in the way. I could take Daniel back a Swiss watch," she added in a breezy tone.

"You're welcome to come," he shot back. "You ought to be able to find something suitable for your devoted fiancé."

She ignored the sarcasm. "Good. When do we go?"

"Now. I suppose you want to go back to the room first?"

She shook her head. "Ready when you are."

The confines of the car were more than Caitlin had bargained for. It was impossible to sit so close to Jake and not be affected. Heading north with the Alps bearing down on them, they encountered even more fog and mist than in Como. It made no difference, she reflected. Nothing did. They were stopped at the border but it was a cursory inspection, with both answering questions about citizenship.

They reached Lugano, and after a couple of wrong turns, Jake pulled into a modern, open-air parking garage, finding a space on the third level.

"My appointment at the hotel isn't for a while ," he said breaking a lengthy silence. "We can kill some time in a Swiss department store, if you like."

For an hour or so, Caitlin explored the various levels of the modern structure, finding some small gifts for her family and choosing a new lipstick for herself. Jake had disappeared soon after their entrance. It was just as well.

He reappeared some time later as she was about to exit the store with no explanation of where he'd been. As they left, Jake spotted a jewelry store across the street.

"I want to take a look. You haven't found anything for your fiancé yet have you?" His tone indicated he was in a black mood, had been since she mentioned buying a gift for Daniel.

Caitlin shook her head. "I've changed my mind about buying him a watch." No need to tell Jake she wouldn't be seeing Daniel again much less giving him a present.

Jake pursed his mouth as if he'd just bit into something acrid. "Well, jewelry might be just the thing for my mother," he said and took her arm to cross the busy street, as always his touch unsettling her.

They stood outside the window of the small, exclusive shop admiring a display of gold chains, some evening watches and a tray of ornate dinner rings.

"Anything there that catches your eye?" he asked, his tone somewhat lighter.

" I don't know your mother's taste, but I always think something simple is best. A special occasion?"

"Her birthday—next month," he responded gruffly and pointed to the tray of rings. "Those are all very fancy."

"Except for the bottom row. That one's perfect. Look at the color." She pointed to a modest-sized sapphire of brilliant color flanked by tiny diamonds.

"Not very big."

"It's beautiful. Simple, yet elegant," Caitlin murmured not adding that its main attraction was that the sapphire matched Jake's eyes and was about as far as possible from the huge pear-shaped diamond that had been Daniel's idea of what a ring should look like. "But, rather than a dinner ring, I am afraid it looks more like an...an.."

"An engagement ring?" Jake finished for her.

She nodded, suddenly aware that Jake was going to buy it for Jenny. "Are you going to go in?"

"I was. Bibi might like a new watch. She's hard on them. Always knocking them on her gardening tools. I'll take a closer look inside."

Caitlin was not about to go in and watch him buy a ring for Jenny. "Do you mind if I dash back into the department store? I need some shampoo," she said, her voice strained. Without waiting for his answer, she darted back across the street and into the store.

He was waiting for her when she came back out carrying her purchase in a small nondescript bag. "Find anything?" she asked.

"A watch." Again his voice was cold. "I've got to hurry if I'm going to make it to the hotel on time."

He made it sound as if she were to blame for his being late when she had only been in the store for 5 minutes.

The small inn, on the outskirts of the city, had some charm, but it was clear that it was in need of major renovations and the area surrounding it was less than inviting.

"You can sit in the lobby while I talk to the owners," Jake said in a peremptory manner. "I'll ask them to send you something to drink, and we can have lunch afterward."

Caitlin had had enough of his officious manner. "I'd rather sit in the car. I bought a magazine."

"Suit yourself," he shot back in testy fashion making her feel almost sorry for the hapless Jenny.

Jake disappeared inside and Caitlin attacked the Italian fashion magazine, furious at his treatment of her. Who did he think he was? She turned page after page with little interest in the styles, then turned to the window to gaze unseeing at the dreary landscape.

Caitlin wondered how often Jake had to be away from home. If she were married to him, she would want to go with him whenever possible. Like Mrs. Croft, the admiral's wife in *Persuasion* who had sailed the high seas with her husband. Would Jenny want to travel with Jake? The prospect was something that didn't bear thinking about.

Jake was back in a very short time, going to the trunk to get the camera and then returning to her open window. "The place needs far too much work. However, I told Harry I'd get a shot of it to show him. Go up next to the sign. It will give us a better perspective."

Caitlin protested. After the way he'd been acting, she owed him no favors. When she didn't move, Jake put the camera on the hood of the car and yanked open the car door.

One hand under her elbow, he hauled her resisting form out. "Over there, please." he said , but it wasn't a request, it was an order.

Caitlin, raging, gave him a push. She tore free, took one step and stumbled. Jake grabbed her, retrieving her with a speed that caused her to fall back against him.

She heard him groan and knew his arms were supportive not forceful. For a second she thought he was going to kiss her again. "You bring out the absolute worst in me, Caitlin Harris. Forgive me."

Just then a teenage boy approached them. He'd spotted the camera on the hood and took a look at them, apparently coming to the conclusion they were in a lovers' embrace. He glanced again at the camera and turned to Jake, asking if he'd like their picture taken in front of their honeymoon hotel. They both stared at the young man. Then Jake started to laugh. "If you would, please!"

The boy, no more than 15, took several shots of them in front of the hotel next to the sign. Jake thanked him, accepted the return of the camera and opened the door for Caitlin.

There was silence on the return trip, Caitlin alternating between numbness and fury, Jake staring straight ahead on the road.

After some distance, he spoke. It's nearly lunch time. Interested?"

"Not with you," she muttered under her breath. She was not sure he heard it, but then he said in a jibing manner.

"Thinking of the almost honeymoon, I suppose. Missing the boyfriend…"

Caitlin turned on him, sputtering. "Don't mention Daniel to me. He may be inconsiderate, even a jerk at times, but compared to you he's a…a…a paragon." Jake snorted. There was no other word for it. His eyes glittered as he looked over at her and an expression so dark crossed his face that she drew back, but only for a moment.

"This is the end of the road for us." She met his stare without flinching. "I'm sure you can find a room in Milan. Cities aren't quite as filled up in the holiday season as the resort towns. Milan is only a half hour or so away, so you won't be too inconvenienced. And traveling with you, I'm afraid, creates more problems than it solves."

He continued to stare at her, then said, "We have to talk about it."

"There's nothing to talk about," she said and lapsed into arctic silence as the Mercedes continued to eat up the miles back to Cernobbio and the hotel. But there was much to think about if only she could get her addled brain straightened out.

"Caitlin," Jake said at last in an even tone. "I have…several extremely important calls coming to the Villa Regina. You might call them urgent. I, uh, am afraid that if I leave now, I'll miss them and…"

"Business calls?"

"Yes."

She took her time answering, although she had arrived at her shameful conclusion moments before. Caitlin hated him. Hated Jake.

But she hated herself more—for being so weak where he was concerned. She wanted him near her as long as she could have him and the devil be damned. She'd already figured out that he was not a violent man and that he did have control over himself despite the outbursts that she helped incite.

"All right." She heard an audible sigh of relief and wished for a similar peace. But, no, she had doomed herself to another week of the most futile of exercises.

They spent the rest of the trip in stilted conversation, speaking to each other only when necessary.

Jake decided to stop in Como before going on to the hotel. He had a couple of errands to run, he said, without explaining what they were, and again Caitlin chose to wait in the car.. She saw him disappear into what was apparently an office building, then coming out fairly quickly he went into an adjacent bank.

It was late afternoon by the time they reached the Villa Regina. Caitlin went up to the rooms alone as Jake said he wanted to see the concierge about directions for the following day along with some other matters.

Caitlin unlocked the door to their suite knowing that the day had taken its toll emotionally. Jake certainly had a lot of irons in the fire. He was close-mouthed about it, almost mysterious. She was crazy not to have stuck by her earlier resolution that they split. If she had, he would have been out of her life by now.

She let herself into the suite, went directly out to the balcony to sit in hopes that the beautiful view would ease her mind. Jake came in shortly, announced he was taking a shower and that he had some other business downstairs. Afterward, if she wanted to, they could search out a place for dinner.

The invitation, proffered in so half-hearted a manner, depressed her further. Her instinct was to spend as much time as possible in his company, but her pride intervened.

"We don't have to spend every minute in each other's pocket," she said, hoping he would protest. "I think I'll just go to the dining room tonight on my own. See you later or in the morning."

He gave her a piercing look, his mouth in a tight line. "If that's what you want," he said and grabbing some clothes from his closet went to the bathroom, slamming the door behind him. So much for his reformed behavior!

Caitlin stayed on the balcony, heart heavier than ever. It was as if she and Jake were truly on a honeymoon—a newly married couple in the throes of battle. She remembered a friend telling her how her own wedding trip had been miserable, a week in which exhaustion, anticipation and frustration had combined to keep them at each other's throats.

She heard him whistle a tuneless fragment as he walked through the bedroom and, shortly after, he left the suite without so much as a word to her.

Without enthusiasm, she showered, dressed and prepared to go downstairs. They'd skipped lunch and it was too early to be served in the hotel dining room given the Italians' custom of a late evening meal. But she'd give it a try. If not, there was some cheese left in the frigo bar. When the phone rang, she leaped toward it, her heart soaring. It must be Jake wanting her to meet him downstairs. But it was not Jake..

"Caitlin. It is Francesca." The Italian girl's voice sounded as if she were nearby.

"I'm in the lobby," she said confirming Caitlin's hunch.

"In the lobby?" Caitlin repeated incredulously .

"Nico and I. We have been worried about you since you left so quickly in the middle of the night. We drove up from Milan to take you to dinner if you are free. May we come up?"

"You and Nico," Caitlin said, her voice cool. She thought she had taken leave of them permanently. What a horrendous situation that had been. She never wanted to see either of them again."

"We have something for you. Something you left behind," Francesca said. "It looks valuable. Well, perhaps sentimental value. A medal I think.

"Oh, no," Caitlin gasped horrified. Her grandmother's St. Christopher medal. Gran had bestowed it upon Caitlin before she left saying she would be safe in her solitary travels. Her sailor grandfather had given it to her grandmother 50 years before. Said it had kept him safe on the high seas, and now it would protect Caitlin her grandmother said.

She must have taken it out of her purse in the bedroom in Milan searching for something else and forgot to put it back in. Or more likely it had been dumped out when Signora Carli had upended Caitlin's bag! In her haste to leave the apartment she had overlooked it. There was nothing to do but meet with them.

"Yes, please come up," she said, and gave them the suite number. She'd deal with turning down the dinner invitation after she got her medal. Had Nico not made an ass of himself she wouldn't have left in such a hurry. She owed them nothing. Still....

She had no sooner hung up when she heard noise in the outer room and soon Jake was tapping on the bedroom door. He stuck his head in. "I didn't think you really wanted to be alone all evening....There's a restaurant in Piazza Cavour the concierge recommended. Second story overlooking the lake ..."

"But I won't be by myself," Caitlin countered unwisely. "Francesca and Nico Carli are on their way up here. They've asked me to go to dinner." No need to tell him she had no intention of going.

Jake came in, staring at her incredulously. "Are you completely crazy that you would have anything to do with those two?" His face grew so stormy she worried he might have a fit as he continued. "My God, they should have been reported to the authorities! First that young goat made advances endangering your welfare. Then the parents falsely accuse you of theft and, seduction."

Jake paused, gathering steam. "And perhaps the most egregious offense of all, allowing you, a young single woman, to leave their home in the middle of the night in a strange city, a strange country, and go sit the night in a train station where anything could have happened to you."

He took a breath and went on, "As for that...that... idiot of a sister. I don't know if she's a tart or just an awful flirt, but how could you have anything to do with them?"

Jake's tirade was interrupted by a knock on the door His face near livid before, now grew black with fury..

"I'll get it.." Caitlin started to say, worried about what Jake might do.

"Oh, no you won't. I've got a few things to say to that couple."

And with that he marched into the sitting room, Caitlin right behind him as he yanked open the door.   It was clear from their faces that whatever the brother and sister had expected, it was not this avenging angel.

"Caitlin?" Francesca had suddenly become hesitant. Nico slunk behind his shorter sister in a patently unsuccessful ploy to hide.

"Come in. I've a few things to say to you two!" Jake slammed the door and rounded on them. "How dare you two show your faces here. Have you no pride, no decency?"

"We…we came to apologize for the other night," Francesca began, and quickly dug into her pocket and came forth with the medal, "and to return this to Caitlin which she forgot when she left the flat."

"Left the flat? That's a good one. You mean when she was driven out of the flat!"   yelled Jake and took the medal out of her hand and handed it to Caitlin.

"What kind of people turn a young guest into the street at 3 a.m. and falsely accuse her of theft? I know people from one end of this country to another, and I can tell you that not one of them, no one I've ever met in Italy, would have acted as your family did. Despicable!"

And then suddenly he seemed to remember Nico's part in that fateful evening. He elbowed Francesca out of the way and moved toward the young man, towering over him. "And you, you worthless … I'd like to give you what you deserve.."

From her vantage point, Caitlin could see Nico turn pale. For once Francesca was speechless.   Caitlin snapped out of her trance and moved quickly between Nico and Jake, fearful that the enraged Jake would do bodily harm to the younger man.

But Nico surprised her. He coughed once, twice from nervousness and probably fear, and addressed her in his impressive English. "No, Signorina. I must take my—how do you say it—my licks. I behaved abominably the other night. As perhaps you can tell, I cannot hold my wine. It is a big failing, especially for an Italian."

Nico gave a sorry little smile before going on. "I am sorry for behaving as I did and being the cause of your flight into the street. It is true we all behaved without honor.

"My father asked I convey his sincerest apologies as well. He had just learned that a friend of his had been gravely injured in an accident and he was not thinking clearly. Please, Signorina, please tell me you forgive me, and forgive my family for the way we acted." She noticed he said nothing about his mother, the she-tiger.

Caitlin stared at Nico so obviously distraught. She paused for a moment, then said quietly, "I do forgive you. I hope your father's friend..."

Nico shook his head, his eyes sad. "He was piloting his own plane. There was little hope at the outset..."

But Jake was not so conciliatory. He turned on Caitlin. "You forgive HIM?" Jake trumpeted. "You forgive him!!"

"Enough!" Caitlin turned her back on Nico and confronted Jake. " I said that's enough. And I do mean enough." Her decisive voice took him by surprise.

Caitlin turned to Francesca. "Thank you for returning my medal. It is my grandmother's and you are right, it does have great value to me. I very much appreciate your making the trip. Thank you also for the dinner invitation, but I am unable to accept. Now if you will both excuse me. I...I have a headache and I am going to rest." And with that she turned and went into the bedroom and shut the door leaving the two unfortunate people to Jake.

They must have left quietly and quickly for she heard the door shut and then nothing else. She was not sure but what Jake had escorted them down to the lobby, but after a few minutes she heard noises in the outer room.

Grabbing her night clothes, she went into the bathroom and locking the door behind her, began to draw a long, hot bath. If ever there was a night for a calming soak, this was it. Trying to relax , she could feel her heart pounding in her chest. It would be a long while before she would be able to sleep.. Perhaps later she'd call room service and ask for hot milk or whatever potion the Italians used when in turmoil.

"

Chapter 10

It was a subdued pair who met the next morning in the breakfast room, Jake overly polite and solicitous, Caitlin, withdrawn and pale from lack of sleep. She stared out the window onto Lake Como, the mist already starting to rise.

"It's a beautiful day, the clearest morning we've had," Jake murmured as he sat down at the table. Caitlin nodded. "It would be an ideal time to take a boat ride around the lake if you're interested."

Caitlin looked up into the deep blue eyes and saw a disarming, if sheepish, expression cross his face.

"Why not?" she answered, immune now, she convinced herself, to his considerable charm. It was either that or pack up and go home. She was at his mercy as far as sightseeing went. Without a car there was little she could do in this quiet resort.

Before arriving in Europe, she had thought she wouldn't mind being without a male escort. She had changed her mind. A woman on her own in this part of the world was too often subject to unwelcome attention, the least objectionable being the target of male stares. Number one example: the unfair characterization and attack by the mother of Francesca and Nico Carli.

She turned her gaze to the lake once more as she sipped her morning *caffe latte*. Jake Riordan had shown his true colors last night. Thank God he didn't have any younger sisters. They wouldn't have been allowed to even talk to a boy. And to think she had thought the Italians protective of their women. They didn't hold a candle to Jake Riordan. Maybe there was some Italian in his background.. Not that she was his woman, but he had obviously made it his mission to see over her until she went home.

"Caitlin!" She had been woolgathering. She turned to him, expectant.

"I'll sign us up for a boat tour, then?"

She nodded, murmured, "Fine," in a voice devoid of emotion.

It was a memorable ride around the Y-shaped Lago di Como, the clear atmosphere providing perfect views of the magnificent villas and colorful, formal gardens ringing the water. Above, the snow-capped Alps loomed high while white sails dotted the shimmering blue water.

Conversation between them was at a minimum until they approached Villa d'Este, the palace built by a Cardinal Gallio, son of Lucretia Borgia, in the 16th century, now the most superior of hotels.

They had viewed it from the road on their drive up the west coast, but the perspective from the water gave far more indication of the scope and elegance of the palatial building and the magnificent gardens in which it sat.

"It must cost a bundle to stay there," Caitlin murmured.

"But worth every penny."

"You've stayed there?"

"Once. The kind of place you pick for a very special occasion."

"An experience worth repeating?"

"Definitely. One I hope I won't have long to wait for."

Caitlin pretended to be interested in a passing boat. His meaning was all too clear. Jake meant to bring Jenny here on their honeymoon."

She was silent for much of the remainder of the trip, occasionally taking a photo of an especially picturesque villa. Eventually. they spotted Bellagio, one of several resort towns on the lake, and Caitlin could not hide her enthusiasm.

Jake, picking up eagerly on any such interest on her part, suggested they drive there for dinner. "We could go up the west side of the lake to Cadenabbia where a ferry will take us across. Or we can go down to the city of Como and drive up the east coast."

"Drive," said Caitlin without hesitation. "I've been looking at the mountain from our balcony for three days now. I'd like a closer look."

"And the lady shall have one." Jake's sigh of relief was audible. Caitlin shot him a quick glance. Just because she was being civil, didn't mean she was going to revert to her former compliant self.

They began their trip to Bellagio a little after 6 p.m., driving down to Como and starting up the eastern shore. Less than half an hour later, Caitlin had seen more of the lake road than she wanted. Gripping the arm rests of the Mercedes, she tried stifling the little yelps that came to her lips as they found themselves in what amounted to a rush hour traffic marathon..

The narrow shore road hugged the mountain. Guard rails, where they existed, seemed to be placed without rhyme or reason, and worst of all, huge chunks of asphalt had washed out on the lake side of the pavement.

To Caitlin, it looked as if there was barely enough room for one car. When other vehicles came at them from the opposite direction, Jake had to hug the rock-bound base of the mountain. They had negotiated one such passing when Caitlin let out a real scream. A large tour bus was headed toward them just as the road curved, its speed far from cautious.

Caitlin groaned and glanced at Jake. "And I thought the Autostrada was bad. At least the road was wide there."

Jake's expression was surprisingly calm. "It's going to be all right. We back up until we find a place where its wide enough for the bus to pass us," Jake said and then did so.

"Thank, God, we're on the inside. We could be in the lake if we weren't." Anxiety had loosened her tongue.

"We won't be on the return trip," Jake reminded her.

"We'll take the ferry. We can, can't we?"

"Yes," he said in a calming voice. He glanced over, saw her gripping her hands. "Try to relax."

"I will. I am." She made a concerted effort and succeeded for all of two minutes.

Something alerted her to glance back. "Oh, my God, look behind us." A black squat car almost wider than it was long, was on their tail. The driver was so close she could see the man's face, rigid, intent on getting home.

"The fool!" Jake swore, his own face turning grim. He pulled the Mercedes as far as he could to the right, the base of the mountain a sheer sheet of rock. The black car passed and in a burst of speed disappeared from sight.

Several times in the next half hour the scenario was replayed, workers in Como eager to get to the comfort of their homes and the evening meal.

They pulled into Bellagio, Caitlin in such a state that the beauty of the resort momentarily escaped her. By the time they were sitting in a sedate dining room of an ancient villa overlooking the lake, and sipping their wine she began to inspect the surroundings.

"Look! There's the ferry coming now. We'll be able to take it back."

Jake smiled at her. "It docks right down there." He pointed to the left. Feel better now?"

"I wasn't the only one unhinged. Admit it now. Weren't you just a little bit scared?" Fear had reduced the hostility she had been feeling.

Jake smiled and shook his head.

"What!" she protested.

"I was a whole lot scared," he said. "Crazy drivers all try to prove something."

"Which is?"

"A subject unfit for your innocent ears," he teased.

She hooted, forgetting to be aloof. "Well, if you're talking about masculinity, somebody ought to tell these race car drivers that a lead foot and an empty space between the ears leaves something to be desired."

Jake laughed and poured more wine into her glass. "Here, this is what you need."

He was being his most affable, trying obviously to make her forget the previous evening's hostilities. She wasn't about to, but she could be affable too.

As she took a sip of wine, he murmured, " You bring up an interesting subject, Caitlin. What do you find desirable in a man?"

She steeled herself against the unwelcome rise of emotion within her. "I'm not sure what you mean."

Jake laughed, said softly, "Just what I said. What do you think makes a man sexy? If not the way he drives, then what? His clothes, his job, money, power? Don't tell me you drool over the Adonis types."

She didn't have to think twice. She lifted her glass, put it down without drinking. "Intelligence. Intelligence in a man is very sexy. I never can resist it."

Jake's gaze was warm on her face. He said nothing for a moment. Then, "Daniel's a very intelligent man."

"How would you know?"

For some reason, the abruptness of her question, took him aback. She searched his face, a move which further discomfited him if his return gaze was any indication. His mouth twisted in a wry grin and he played with the silverware before answering smoothly, "It stands to reason. You picked him."

The wine suddenly took effect, making her more effusive. "Daniel is very bright, very smart. About certain things. About business. By the time he's 50, he's going to own half of Hartford."

Jake smiled. "Most dictionaries wouldn't quibble with that definition."

"Intelligence has little to do with manipulation, the ability to stockpile money," she retorted. "It's about insight. Knowing about people. Being able to look inside and see what they care about. What they fear most. What makes them happy."

Caitlin sighed, looked out the expanse of windows seeing nothing. Recklessly she grabbed her refilled glass and drank half of it in one gulp.

Jake took the glass from her and put it down. "I think we both should get some food into us." He looked at her so kindly her eyes filled, and angrily she reached for her purse. *She was not going to let him work his charm on her!* "I'm going to powder my nose," she announced and stalked off.

Jake was, by turns, solicitous and amusing when she returned, obviously not sure what might set her off. Granted she had been a powder keg for days.

Even now in this beautiful place, she could not bring herself to relax. The elegant, staid dining room was only partially filled this time of year, the majority of the diners, elderly. A string duo, flanked by potted palms, played softly .

They were drinking espresso when Jake looked at his watch and then shook it. "What's the time?"

Caitlin looked at hers. "Just 8:30. Why?"

"My watch has stopped."

"What's the matter?"

Instead of answering, he pointed to the ferry just easing out of the dock.

"Yes?"

"The last ferry leaves at 8:30. That's the one. My watch says 8."

"It can't be," she wailed.

Jake tried to soothe her. It's not that bad. The rush hour is over. The buses have probably made their last runs as well."

"If we have to drive that road again, I want to go now while it's still light."

"We've only got a few minutes of daylight left. We'll take it easy."

Barely giving him time to settle the bill, Caitlin dragged him out to the street fronting the lake. There were few cars parked. Most people, arriving by boat, were staying the night, she guessed

"We could stay over, too, "Jake said. "Doubt that they're filled up here."

Caitlin shook her head. With her luck, they'd only be able to get one room with one bed. " Let's go. I promise I won't carry on."

And she was as good as her word the first quarter hour. Rain began to fall, first a sprinkling, then a steady patter than turned into a downpour.

Caitlin hated storms, especially while traveling, especially on this road ."Can't you pull over until it lets up?"

"If I pull over, we're in the lake," Jake said sharply.

"Well, do *something*!"

"I am. I'm driving! And I won't be responsible for what happens if you don't stop the caterwauling."

She moved as far away from him as she could and called him—and herself—every name she could think of—all under her breath. The minute they got back safely at the hotel, she was throwing him out. Forever. If he needed to be in the Villa Regina, he could sleep on one of the sofas in the lobby for all she cared.

They crept along at a snail's pace for about 10 minutes, Jake muttering about the lack of visibility, Caitlin hanging on to the arm rest for dear life.

Suddenly she heard Jake swear. Caitlin, peered through the windshield, screamed as she saw the car coming at them at an unsafe speed. It happened in seconds. The driver apparently tried to stop, started to skid. Jake swerved, and the Mercedes headed down the sloping, unprotected bank toward the lake.

Chapter 11

Preparing to hit the water, Caitlin stifled the scream deep in her throat, tensing as the car hit something and came to a bumpy halt.

"Thank God." She gave a little cry of relief . They were not in the lake.

Jake put a hand on her arm. "Okay?"

"Yes. How far are we from the water?"

"I'll take a look." He found a flashlight in the glove compartment and got out to inspect. "The most beautiful boulder I've ever seen in my life," he called to her. "We're about two feet from the water's edge. Front tire is flat. There might be more damage. I can't tell."

Caitlin peered through the windshield, barely able to see him through the heavy fog. "We need help. What'll we do?" She could not suppress the anxious note in her voice.

"If a car comes along we'll try for a ride into Como." He said nothing about the rock. Probably, Jake, too, feared it could be dislodged by more rain or maneuvering the car.

Not a single vehicle passed their way. Caitlin kept peering out the window, anxiety, fueled by the earlier nerve-wracking ride, taking its toll.

"Isn't there anything we can do?" she wailed.

"You can stop moaning. You're not making things any better."

"And I suppose you are!" She started biting her fingernails, a habit she'd broken when she was 13. Mean, terrible man.

For several long minutes there was silence, Jake peering out through the back window. He turned to her, pointed. "Look. Halfway up the mountain." A light shone dimly through the fog. Must be a cottage, a home of some sort. Want to try it?"

She looked at him. She had on a silk dress with a narrow skirt and was wearing high-heeled sandals, hardly the things in which to go hiking up the wet, presumably slippery mountain."Where are all those cars that were bedeviling us earlier?" she cried.

Jake spoke sharply. "Throwing a fit isn't going to make a car appear."

`   "Who's throwing a fit!" She held up one foot. These high heels aren't exactly made for hiking the foothills of the Alps."

"The only other alternatives are to sit in the car, which might start to move, or stand in the rain in the road and get hit by the first maniac that comes by. I'll carry you on my back if need be." He spoke patiently as if she were a half-wit."

"I'll walk in my stocking feet first."

Jake made a disgusted sound. "Hopefully, they'll have a telephone up there. We can call for help. Come on." He put out a hand and leaving her no choice, pulled her out his door. "Put your wrap over your head. We'll get wet, but we should be inside in 10 or 15 minutes." She did as she told but was soon freezing, their lightweight clothing no match for the cold April rain.

The base of the mountain in front of them was not the sheer rock they had observed earlier, but was covered with low bushes which made it possible to pull themselves up from the road. Clawing their way up, Jake pushing Caitlin from behind, they negotiated the first big obstacle.

The rain had softened to a regular drizzle, and taking Caitlin's hand firmly in his, Jake now began going up the steep slope in a zigzag pattern.

"It's how trains get over mountains. Called a switchback," he explained. Caitlin made a rude noise. Her shoes were impossible, the heels sinking into the soft ground each step she took. Still they managed to plow their way upward steadily, the grassy surface often slippery. At one point she slipped going down on one knee into wet leaves. Jake handed her the flashlight and unceremoniously swung her up into his arms.

"Put me down," she ordered. "I'm too heavy."

"Quiet! If you don't stop thrashing, I'm going to drop you and let you roll down the mountain into the water."

"Jake!"

"Be quiet. Did anybody ever tell you that you can be a giant pain in the behind?"

"At least I'm not an arrogant bully."

"And I am." He slid her abruptly to the ground.

"Good," she said, all haughtiness. "I'll walk the rest of the way."

"We're here, Miss Snip."

"Oh." Caitlin looked up and saw a cottage a short distance away. Built into the side of the mountain, it appeared to have two levels. There was a light in the upper one.

Jake flashed the light in her face. He was even wetter than she, the stole having provided Caitlin some protection despite its inadequacies. The rain had nearly stopped.

"Come on, let's go." He grabbed her hand and started to move, then stopped. "No wait. You've got those little gold hoops in your ears?"

"Yes."

"Take them off."

"What!"

"Hurry up. Put one on your ring finger the way you did that first night in San Margherita," he ordered.

"No. What for?"

"Don't argue with me, dammit." Jake's equanimity had deserted him. "I want to get dried off. So they'll think we're married. That's what for. We're likely to get a better reception if they think you're my wife."

Caitlin sneezed. "Than if they think I'm a loose woman walking around the Alps at night with a strange man? Give me a break."

Jake snorted, explained impatiently, "Italians, especially those in the rural parts, hold strict views about unmarried women. Will you do what I said?"

Caitlin complied, dropping the second earring in her bag, and gave him a stinging look which went unnoticed in the darkness. Jake strode forward and pounded on the door.

It was opened by a boy of about 15 who was plainly dumbfounded to find such bedraggled creatures seeking refuge. He was soon joined by his parents, a red-cheeked, black-eyed sturdy woman in a housedress who clucked sympathetically as she caught sight of their sopping condition and her husband, a giant, who towered over them all.

The lower room, in which they had entered, appeared to be a storage area. They were herded upstairs to the living quarters, a large expanse which served as both dining and living rooms. It was a modest home, scrupulously clean, Caitlin noticed at once.

The Basciani family spoke little English. Without waiting to hear Caitlin's explanation, all three went to work, bringing towels and coffee and begging them to make themselves at home. Jake, silent as Caitlin explained to their hosts what had happened, interrupted. "The telephone. Don't forget to ask."

"It's out," she said quickly after posing the question. "The storm. They tried earlier. Tomorrow, Gianni," she nodded at the boy, "will go get help. A relative will tow the car, if need be, to Como where he has a service station. We can get a ride in the tow truck."

Caitlin went on, giving their hosts a grateful smile. "Signore Basciani manages a farm in the other direction. Another son has their car and is in Milan on a business matter. They are very sorry that all they can offer us tonight is a bed."

"Millie grazie," Jake told the couple and to Caitlin, "Take it. We've got to get out of these clothes." He sneezed loudly as if to emphasize the need, then looked pointedly at her hand. Caitlin followed his gaze, glanced at the gold hoop on her finger, blushed furiously.

Signora Basciani intercepted the look, saw the rising color. "*Gli sposi!*" she cried.

"She thinks we were just married, that I'm a new bride." Caitlin muttered.

"And so you are," said Jake shamelessly and beamed at the couple, the proud bridegroom.

Ignoring the impulse to hit him, Caitlin told the Signora that they would be very grateful if they could stay the night.

There were pleased murmurs from their hosts, offers of food which were refused, and soon Signora Basciani led them to a small curtained alcove at the far end of the large room. She parted the curtains and beckoned them. Caitlin followed with sinking heart, Jake behind her. Not even a room with a door!

Inside was a narrow double bed, a small chest and a straight-back wooden chair. From the chest, the lady of the house withdrew some garments.

She handed Caitlin a nightgown, a white, voluminous tent with embroidered bodice, high neck and long sleeves. A pair of outsized pajamas for Jake was placed on one pillow as Caitlin stared at the bed.

"Don't look like that, she'll notice," Jake muttered. But the Signora smiled tenderly at them perhaps remembering her own entrance into wedded bliss. She explained that their room was at the far side of the house, along with the bathroom, the boy Gianni sleeping in an adjacent loft. They were to call if they needed anything, she said and bid them, "*buono notte.*"

"What are we going to do?" Caitlin had eyes only for the narrow bed.

"For starters you can stop wringing your hands," Jake muttered. "There are two blankets on the bed. I'll take one and sit up in the chair."

"You can't."

"You want the chair?"

"No." She glared at him knowing full well she was being unreasonable in a ridiculous situation.

"You want to share the bed with me?"

"No!"

"Then be quiet and get out of the wet clothes and put on the nightgown. And stop complaining. You're safe and you're dry or you will be as soon as you get out of those things. Where did she say the bathroom was?"

"Down by their rooms. I'm not going to change there and take the chance of somebody seeing me in this."

Jake laughed. "You can't look any worse than you already do. Undress here. I'll turn around."

She turned her back on him, grateful to be further shown what kind of a person he really was. An unfeeling human being was the least of his faults.

Caitlin picked up the nightgown. "Are you turned around?"

"No, I've got my tongue hanging out, waiting for you to…"

She spun around to see that his back was to her and that he was minus his clothes, a foot-long pale strip interrupting the bronze of back and legs.

She spun back, her face hot, and began to peel off the silk dress and the remains of her stockings. She pulled the tent over her head before removing her bra and briefs and draped the wet garments as inconspicuously as she could on the foot of the bed.

"Okay to turn around?" Jake's voice was brusque.

"In a minute." She crawled into bed, then back out, stripping off the outer blanket and placing it at the foot of the bed for him. She climbed in again, murmuring that she was decent.

He turned and she started laughing, the oversized pajamas obviously belonging to Signore Basciani.

"Thanks a lot." He hung his jacket and shirt on the back of the chair, spread his socks on the floor. Caitlin waited until he draped himself in the blanket and sat down on the hard chair before pulling the string attached to the ceiling light.

There was silence, not even a rattle from the other end of the house. The bed was comfortable and slowly Caitlin was getting warm after being half frozen. Jake, she knew, was not faring as well.

She heard him mutter something about their host looking like a scoundrel out of an opera. "Cavaradossi. That's the villain in *Tosca*, right? She could tell he was trying to distract himself.

She giggled in spite of herself, forgetting that she had decided earlier to hate Jake. "No, Scarpia's the bad guy. Cavaradossi is Tosca's lover…" She stopped abruptly, heard what sounded like a snort.

She stretched luxuriously. The bed was decidedly cozy and comfortable. "Warm yet?" she asked.

"All but my feet."

"Put on your socks—oh, they're wet."

"Yes." Sarcasm hung in the air.

She was silent. She could hear him shifting, trying to get comfortable sitting upright in the straight back kitchen chair.

Caitlin closed her eyes, opened them as she heard him muttering.

She sat up. "Jake, this is ridiculous. We're both tired, cold, sleepy."

"What are you trying to say?"

She paused trying to gauge what the consequence of her words would be. "There's room for both of us in the bed. You keep to your side and I'll keep to mine."

The laugh was dry, humorless. "Don't tell me the proper Signorina Harris has thoughts for the lowly chauffeur."

"Come on. Don't be stubborn. You can stick to the other side of the bed."

"This from the girl who less than a week ago thought it immoral to share a suite with me."

"I'm safe," she said drily. "One scream and I'll have three rescuers in here pronto."

She could tell he was wavering. A huge sneeze broke the silence, then the room was quiet again. Still he didn't move.

"Jake?" He didn't answer. Stubborn idiot. She got up and whipping the remaining blanket off the bed wrapped it around her.

"What are you doing?"

"If you won't sleep up here, then neither can I. I'll sleep on the floor.

"I've already thought of it. There's nothing but a scatter rug. Not even big enough to cushion your backside."

"If you persist in being pig-headed, so will I."

He hesitated, and she lay down on the floor, gasping at the cold hardness.

She heard him move and suddenly the alcove was full of light. Wrapped in his blanket, Indian style, he squatted down with a dour look. "How did I ever get mixed up with a nutty female like you?"

"Come here." He held out a hand, and she took it, untangling herself from the wool coverlet. He spread his blanket on the bed, put her blanket on top of it, then cast her nightgown a glance.

"Talk about sexpots," he muttered and gave her a look that started her giggling.

"Get in," he ordered, and when she obeyed, he pulled the light string, and she felt the mattress depress under his weight.

Caitlin was too tired from the climb to be nervous. It was anything but a romantic situation. She looked like a drowned rat, and Jake was a crab. She hugged her side of the bed and realized Jake was doing the same. She could hear him breathing evenly, a sign he was sleeping.

She sighed. Her feet were freezing. What she wouldn't give for a pair of thick socks. Or to be able to put her feet--on Jake's! She could feel the heat radiate from him. The bed sloped a little from Jake's weight, and she had a hard time keeping to her side. But at least they weren't at each other's throats anymore. And she was glad she was over him, the physical attraction dissolving in the spats they kept having.

She started to slide and slip to the center of the bed, and sensing a delicious pool of warmth, pulled herself back, then fell asleep.

Caitlin felt herself sliding, sliding down the mountainside, but it was warm and dry instead of cold and wet. And instead of Lake Como at the end, there was the boulder, an immovable force, warm, fragrant—with arms.

She roused, only half awake. She was nestled against Jake, her head on his chest, his scent and warmth mesmerizing, his arms around her.

"Jake," she said softly. His answer was to tighten his hold on her, waking her completely.

Shock kept her immobile, fear silent. She tried to free herself from Jake's clutch without waking him, but without success.

He woke as she tried to pull away, instantly aware of the situation, and he groaned. "Oh, the hell with it! I can stand it any longer."

" My God , I've dreamed of this forever," he muttered in the darkness. "Cait, you must have guessed…right from the start." And in a second he had pulled her on top of him, his mouth moving over her face and the half inch of bare neck not covered by the nightgown.

She was thoroughly awake at last and in a state of paralysis. "Jake, oh, Jake. We can't do this. It's not right."

"I know, darling." His voice was soothing. "But I can't stand it any longer, Caitlin. I've tried so hard to keep my distance. But, oh, Cait, sweetheart."

He kissed her full on the mouth, sending delightful sensations through her. She moved her lips to his chin, while he feasted on the tiny bare patch of her neck. "Damn this tent."

An adolescent giggle escaped her, and one lean hand moved down her back, and under the covers, gently swatted the roundest part of her. Her "Oww" ended in laughter. Jake groaned and took her mouth again.

It lasted mere seconds, Caitlin's damnable conscience sticking its nose in where it wasn't wanted. Was it possible for two people to fall in love in less than week? She had asked herself that question too many times, and the answer had come back each time: When it was Jake Riordan, yes. It was more than physical. Deep down she knew he was the kind of person one could trust as Signora DeLuca had asserted back at the Fiorito.

She pulled away, moved back to kiss him quickly, so he would know her reluctance, pulled away again.

"Jenny," she told Jake. "We can't."

"It's no use. I'm going to call her. Tell her it won't work. Caitlin, darling, it's been you from the start, since I saw you standing on the balcony at the Fiorito. Haven't you guessed? Nobody could mean to me what you do."

Joy blazed through her. "Oh, Jake, do you mean it?" She moved back to him, covered his face with little kisses. It was his turn to pull away. "What is it, Jake? What's the matter?"

"Daniel. We'll have to tell Daniel," he rasped. "Cait, there's something I have to tell you. Something important..."

"Shhh, later. You can tell me everything later. Oh, Jake, dearest...."

"But, Caitlin..." She stopped his words in the only way possible. He groaned and hauled her back onto his chest, pulled at the high neck of the nightgown. "This blasted thing. It's worse than a strait jacket." He moaned again, a man defeated. "All those tiny buttons. It's even starched. So are the pajamas."

She laughed, kissed him again.

He responded with fervor, then pulled back and gently placed his palm over her mouth. "No door and the walls are thin, sweetheart," he explained, his words like a dash of cold lake water...

With difficulty, she slid out of his arms and over the side of the bed. She stood up before Jake knew what was happening.

"Caitlin! What are you doing?" She could hear him fumbling for the light string. Giving it a yank, he lit up the room.

She sat down on the bed. "Jake, darling, you're right. We have to stop.

He swore under his breath, exasperation and disbelief contorting his features. "I don't believe this. How are we going to get through the rest of the night?"

It was Caitlin's move. "This way." She slipped the pillow from under his head, took hers and put both of them lengthwise down the middle of the bed. "Now I can't slide into you." She crawled back in, gazed at him with love, leaned over to lightly kiss his scowling mouth, then lay down on her side of the bed.

Jake swore again, pounded the mattress with his fist.

"I can't believe I'm doing this."

He reached for her, kissed her with new fierceness, then pushing her away, turned out the light and lay on his back, muttering into the darkness.

Chapter 12

They left the Basciani cottage the next morning in the tow truck. Caitlin was half sitting on Jake's lap in the crowded cab. Their hosts waved goodbye, shouting instructions to Marco, the driver, a distant cousin on the Signora's side, to take good care of their new friends. In addition to fixing the flat, some alignment needed to be made. Signor Basciani recommended it be towed before driving.

A broadly smiling Gianni stood between his parents, now nearly the height of his father with the help of his new cowboy boots.

Jake had tried to pay the family for their generous hospitality which had included a breakfast of eggs cooked with leeks and special herbs plus fresh, crusty bread, warm from the stone oven in the nearby field. When they had refused, Jake and Gianni had gone to the car via a nearby lane that he and Caitlin had overlooked in the fog and rain, and taken out the boots and camera.

The ecstatic youth had pressed the boots to his chest explaining in language even Jake could understand that he was a fan of spaghetti Westerns.

Standing on the muddy embankment, he took off his shoes and slipped on the boots, declaring them a perfect fit. A round of picture-taking followed back at the cottage along with an exchange of addresses. Jake, explaining why he needed the hat, had promised to send Gianni a Stetson, as well.

"You've made one young man very happy," Caitlin murmured, her elevated seat allowing her to graze Jake's ear surreptitiously with her mouth.

Jake's arms tightened about her waist. "I'm more interested in making a certain young woman very happy," he whispered back.

Caitlin, in a haze of happiness, colored, and seeing Marco was busy shaking his fist at a slow-going car in front of them, took the opportunity to press her lips against Jake's neck.

She had not been fast enough. Marco shot Jake a knowing grin. Caitlin went from pink to bright red. Jake laughed and kissed her back, full on the mouth, eliciting an encouraging exclamation from Marco.

"You'd better get used to it," Jake whispered. "I can't keep my hands off you," to which Marco gave another shout despite the whisper and the fact that supposedly he didn't understand a word of English.

Caitlin turned to look out the window until her face cooled. She had awakened to find a pillow under her head. Jake, fully dressed in his wrinkled, but now dry clothes, was sitting on the side of the bed.

"Get up, love," he urged huskily, "the day's awastin'." He dropped a kiss on her mouth. "The Signora has coffee ready."

"Just let me get dressed," she said and sat up to run a finger over his mouth.

He grinned, a glint in his eye. "I'm not stopping you."

"I'm not getting up until you leave."

Jake's eyebrows raised in mock horror. "The Signora will think it unfitting. A new bride not permitting her husband in the bedroom while she dresses."

"The Signora will put it down to nerves," Caitlin had retorted, thinking the Signora would be absolutely right. Caitlin was out of her depth.

Pulling herself back to the present, she stared at the lake, calm and beautifully blue in the aftermath of the storm.

Jake and Caitlin. Caitlin and Jake. Was there ever a more beautiful phrase? She had yearned for Jake from almost the start of the relationship. She could pinpoint the moment when it had happened. The first night in San Margherita at the restaurant—just before he had shown her the picture of Jenny.

Jenny. That was the only difficult part. Caitlin hoped she would not be hurt. The way Jake described his and Jenny's relationship, they had cared about each other, but had not been in love—not the way Caitlin and Jake were. Jake also seemed to think that Caitlin had some feeling for Daniel, but she was going to explain that her former fiancé had never meant to her what Jake did.

Jake broke into her thoughts. "There's Como ahead. Now to Marco's station. It was a piece of luck our hosts having a relative in the business and knowledgeable about the Mercedes. He says it won't take long, we can go have lunch, and when we're through, he'll be finished with the car.."

Caitlin smoothed out her wrinkled dress and cast an eye on her still damp shoes, hoping the restaurant would accept her as she was.

"You look beautiful," Jake said, and the light in his eyes started her pulses fluttering. She knew they were both thinking about the same thing—the time when they would be alone in their hotel suite.

They pulled into the service station a few minutes later. Assuring them he would take good care of the car, Marco directed them to a trattoria on the next block, telling Caitlin to explain that he had sent them. On their way to the station they had passed a photo shop, and Jake had pulled out an undeveloped roll of film from the glove compartment and dropped it in Caitlin's purse. Now she took it out along with the disposable camera. Passing the shop on their way to the trattoria, they stopped and left both with a promise of pictures in an hour.

In the small trattoria, they sat side by side holding hands, looking at each other. The excellent minestra and rolls along with a sampling of pork loin the proprietor recommended were barely tasted. The other patrons, mostly local residents, went unnoticed in their self-absorption

They talked about the previous night's storm, the fact that the car was not damaged severely, their good fortune in finding the Basciani home, the look on Gianni's face when Jake had given him the cowboy boots.

They talked of the difficult week it had been. When they had begun to realize there was more than physical attraction between them. How their families would take the news. Again, the subject of Jenny, came up, causing Caitlin anxiety.

"Your mother. She's so fond of Jenny."

"She'll still be fond of her. She'll love you," Jake assured her. Caitlin wasn't so sure.

Ultimately the topic, if unspoken, came back to their being alone. Caitlin knew it was uppermost in Jake's mind, too. She could see it in his eyes, in the way he kept touching her, brushing a tendril off her forehead, running the back of one finger down her cheek, touching his lips to her ear under pretext of speaking.

It was a little more than an hour later when Marco arrived to tell them the car was ready. "Better than before," he assured them in what was apparently a stock phrase at the service station. On their return walk to the station, they stopped at the photo shop and picked up the developed pictures. Caitlin started to glance at them, but then thought better of it. They would look at them together at their hotel, examining the record of their trip together.

Marco turned out to be right, Jake saying that the vintage car ran even more smoothly than before. The short trip to Cernobbio and the Villa Regina was a matter of a few minutes. As he pulled into a parking spot in front of the hotel, Jake pointed out the hotel logo on the front of the building. "We don't have a picture here. Shall we?"

She nodded and retrieved his camera from the glove compartment along with the packets of newly developed photos. Jake cast around for someone to take shots of them in front of the sign. A bellboy who had just stowed luggage into an adjacent car was tapped, and Jake got out the Stetson, placing it on Caitlin's head, then his, while the amused bellboy snapped away. He smiled in approval as they put arms around each other's waist.

"Honeymoon, si?"

"Si," said Jake smiling and tipped him and then put the hat and camera back in the car trunk. With an arm around her waist, he headed Caitlin toward the lobby. She began leafing through the photos unable to wait to see how many they had of Jake with the boots on. I was worried we didn't have any of you wearing the boots, but here's one at the Fiorito and another in Nice…"

She looked up at him through a haze of love. "I'm going to miss those boots. They were my very first impression of you."

Jake laughed, said in a husky voice, "I'll replace it with a more memorable one," causing her color to heighten. What had she ever done to deserve somebody like Jake? Kind, caring, funny and as attractive as any man she had ever seen.

His arm about her waist tightened, and for a second she leaned her head against his shoulder, no longer caring who might see them or what anyone might think.

"*Caitlin!*"

For a second she thought she had heard wrong.

"*Caitlin!*"   This time there was no mistaking her name.

She turned. So did Jake. For a moment she could not see the caller, a cluster of men in business suits blocking her view. The men moved, Jake swore vehemently, and the dozen photos in Caitlin's hand fell with a splash onto the sea of marble.

The first thing that crossed her mind was that in three years, she had never seen this much emotion on Daniel's features. Her ex-fiancé prided himself on his poker face.

Anger, surprise and contempt vied for supremacy as Daniel Sloane went down on one knee in front of them to retrieve the fallen photos.

It was Caitlin who found her voice first. *"Daniel, what are you doing here?"* Jake's arm stayed where it was, his fingers biting into her waist.

"Hello, Caitlin." Daniel righted himself, looked at Jake, his gaze focusing on Jake's arm around Caitlin.

"How's it going, Jake?" His voice was heavy with sarcasm. "Oh, don't bother to answer. I can see for myself. Looks like you hit the jackpot." Daniel's smooth voice was harsh with anger, his face disdainful, as he took in their wrinkled clothing. "Been out all night, I see."

Caitlin and Jake both started to speak, but Daniel wasn't listening.

His gaze raked Caitlin's face. "After I got your fax…"

"I didn't send a fax…"

Daniel sent daggers at Jake. "I didn't think so…"

Jake found his voice. "Hold on a minute," he interrupted. "It's not what it looks like, Daniel. Have you talked to Paolo?"

"Oh, yes!" More sarcasm. "I talked to Paolo all right. He was as confused as I as to what's been going on."

Caitlin stared from Daniel to Jake back to Daniel, suspecting, then rejecting what her mind was telling her. Paolo. They both knew Paolo. "You two know each other?"

Caitlin heard a snort, but this time it wasn't Jake. Daniel, head down, leafing through the photos, answered.

"We roomed together for our first year at college. I use the word loosely but we've been "friends" ever since. I thought I knew old Jake here. I can see I didn't. Looks like you two have had a wonderful time," Daniel added in a patently false pleasant tone.

"You really stumbled on something, didn't you, Jake? And all under the guise of helping me."

Caitlin blanched. It was impossible. She turned to the man at her side to scour his face."Jake?" When he didn't answer immediately she repeated his name. "What's this all about?"

Jake's face was impassive, his voice calm, ignoring Daniel to speak directly to Caitlin. "I can explain. I thought you'd resent me, Caitlin, if you knew I was keeping an eye on you. Daniel called Paolo in Rome after you left, asking him to check and see that you were all right."

"As it happened, I'd just arrived in Rome," Jake continued. "Was there with Paolo for the reopening of his hotel when he got Daniel's call. Paolo thought it necessary one of us go to Portofino to make sure you were all right. Paolo couldn't leave with the hotel reopening, so I was tapped. Paolo knew Signora DeLuca at the Fiorito and managed to get me a room."

Jake looked at Daniel who remained silent, if sneering, through Jake's account. Jake turned to Caitlin, continuing in a taut, urgent voice. "We roomed together at Yale—Paolo, Daniel, myself. We got along all right. Later we went our separate ways. We stay somewhat in touch thanks mostly to Paolo. When one needs a favor, well, we help if we can. Going to Portofino was no problem. I'd come to Italy at Paolo's invitation and when he couldn't leave, I offered—reluctantly, I might add. Then, I saw you..."

"Wanted her for yourself," finished Daniel, his voice rising. You know choice goods obviously."

"Apparently better than you do," Jake flung back. They were attracting attention. People were staring. The businessmen were clearly waiting for the next scene.

"Let's go outside," Caitlin pleaded. "On the terrace."

Jake nodded, and he and Caitlin went outside leaving Daniel no choice but to follow. They moved to the far side of the terrace, the two men coming to a halt, ready for trouble.

"Yes, I wanted Caitlin right from the start. But I didn't think I had the right to go after her," Jake said, "not until I found out how you treated her." His voice lowered. "You're not a bad guy, Daniel. The trouble is your ambition always seems to get in the way of your relationships."

"Ha! And that gave you the right to bed her down in every hotel in Italy?" Daniel sneered, holding out the photos. "The evidence is right here."

"Watch your mouth! Not true," Jake grabbed the pictures from Daniel, thrust them at Caitlin."

"Oh, no?" Daniel's thin, pale face was flushed, growing redder by the minute. He turned his fury on Caitlin.

"And you surely gave no sign of being, what shall we say, a loose lady? Or were you just a better actress than I gave you credit for?"

Caitlin gasped in horror as Jake made a fist and hit Daniel in the jaw. Daniel staggered but did not fall down.

Caitlin waved the clutch of photographs at him. "You're wrong, Daniel. We shared the suite in each instance. Not a room. And we didn't do anything, because while I'd already given you back your ring, Jake wasn't sure I still didn't feel something for you. He didn't want to step on your toes."

"Ha!" Daniel's disbelief was clear.

Caitlin took a deep breath and continued as her ex-fiancé smiled nastily. "But the most important reason nothing happened between us is that Jake is engaged—to a girl back home. Her name is Jenny. Jake is going to explain to her what happened…"

Daniel stared at her, then began to laugh as if she'd just said the most hilarious thing. "Jenny? You did say Jenny? Oh, Caitlin you're so gullible." He laughed louder, the sound threatening her equilibrium.

When Daniel spoke there was no trace of amusement in his voice. "You've been duped, Caitlin. Everybody who knows the Riordan brothers knows that Jenny is Harry's girl. Harry was a year ahead of us in school. Jenny's been his girl forever unless you, Jake, stole her away from Harry. You see, Caitlin, Jake isn't interested in settling down. He's a playboy. Charms the girls, then goes on his merry way."

Caitlin felt herself go hot, then very cold as Daniel ranted on, his laughter and words ringing in her ears. Stunned, she turned as if in a dream, met Jake's gaze, waited for him to deny it.

When he didn't, she said quietly, "Have you nothing to say, Jake?"

"What can he say? He's guilty as hell!" Daniel bellowed. Two elderly women walking out onto the terrace took one startled look and backed in through the doors.

Jake ignored Daniel. "I can explain, Caitlin," he said his tone bleak, "but I know you won't listen to anything I say right now."

She found her voice. "You're right, Jake. Don't bother," she heard herself say.

She looked at Daniel, then Jake. "The one thing worse than a selfish, self-absorbed man who thinks only of himself is a ....is a two-timer....and a liar."

Jake and Daniel started to speak at the same time, but she silenced them both with a wave of the hand. "No wonder you got along so well at college. You make a wonderful, self-serving pair. Conceit and deceit personified."

She took a step toward the double French doors that led to the lobby, stopped, turned back. " I'm ashamed to say I ever had anything to do with either of you."

She faced Jake. "Don't bother coming up for your luggage. I'll have it sent to the desk." And she moved quickly past them through the doors to the lobby, oblivious to the chorus of protest that broke the stunned silence.

Chapter 13

At the desk, the clerk gave no evidence that he, as well as everyone else in the vast lobby, knew Caitlin was the cause of the fight between the two Americans. She requested both keys and moved quickly to the elevator, glancing once back at the terrace. Through the long windows she could see the two men, gesturing dramatically, half dancing around each other in prize-fight fashion.

In the suite. she chained the door behind her, threw the keys on the coffee table and discovered she still had the photos in her hand. On the top was one with her and Jake and the Basciani family. She swallowed a sob, and put the photos down next to the keys.

How could she have gone from the heights to the depths in just a couple of minutes? She never wanted to see Jake again, the man she thought she loved and wanted to spend the rest of her life with.

There was a new urgency to her actions as she pulled his suitcase from the closet and began emptying the drawers of the bureau they had shared.

She handled Jake's clothes as if they were hot coals and flung the neatly folded piles into the open case. When it filled too quickly, she began jamming underwear into the upper pockets of the lid.

Jake had stored some small items in one of the pouches of the suitcase. As she stuffed clean socks into it, the outline of the box containing the watch he had bought in Lugano, took shape. The memory of that unhappy day when she feared he might be buying a ring for Jenny taunted her anew. She'd been blind. Blind with love.

Caitlin snapped the bag shut and then getting his suit-carrier from the closet, called down to the desk and asked them to pick up both pieces. In a matter of minutes, a bellboy had come and left, and she hauled out her own suitcases to start packing. She had barely started when she abruptly dropped a pile of lingerie on a chair and threw herself face down across the huge bed.

What a fool she had been! Daniel was right about one thing. She was gullible. And on so many fronts. Not guessing that Jake and Daniel knew each other was the worst. Jake had certainly dropped his guard often enough.

There'd been the time at the train station in Como. His suitemate, Danford Jones, he'd said, stumbling over the name. Before that, there was the fax he'd sent, the telephone calls and the various comments. And for an hotelier purportedly in Europe to look for acquisitions, he hadn't seemed particularly interested in them.

Her suspicions had been swept aside—because she'd been too eager to be lulled. Hoodwinked. Jake had made a fool of her. Humiliation washed over her anew.

How clever Jake had been pretending he was engaged. He'd been intent on having his cake and eating it too. It hadn't been too difficult to get Caitlin to succumb to his charms. In fact, he'd had to hold her off, she reflected bitterly and thought of the times it had been Jake who had pulled away from her. Until last night when it was she who called a halt...

Tonight Jake had planned on...their being together...in this room. He'd promised to set it straight with Daniel and Jenny. Now Caitlin knew he'd simply planned on leaving her at the end of the trip, no excuses, no commitment. Jake would probably have told her that Jenny wouldn't let him go. If it hadn't been for Daniel, Caitlin would never have known that Jenny was Jake's brother's girl.

She raged inside, hating herself for her naiveté, for her vulnerability. She refused to cry. He wasn't worth it.

Downstairs she had called Jake a liar and a cheat. But, he was worse. He was a thief. He had stolen her self-respect, her peace of mind, her heart.

She flung herself on the bed once more and this time let the storm come. She cried for what had happened, what might have been. Even for the children they might have had.

She had put herself to sleep last night thinking of them—the little girls with glossy brown pigtails, the boys with dark blue, mischievous eyes—to take her mind off the fact that Jake was dangerously close, a mere pillow away.

Finally, her eyes red and swollen, her emotions spent, she slept. It was dusk, almost dark, when she awoke. She sat up to peer out the French doors and saw the mountain lit with a thousand lamps shining from homes. Homes with happily married couples and laughing children, she thought.

Caitlin went to the balcony wondering if she could pick out the Basciani cottage but knew it was futile, and she closed the doors and the drapes, shutting out the twinkling fairy lights. And once more, she began the task of packing.

She made several more trips between dresser and suitcases and caught sight of her disheveled hair and swollen eyes in the mirror above the chest of drawers. She was on her way to splash cold water on her face when she heard the rap on the door.

She made her way briskly across the living room. It wouldn't be Jake. He wouldn't dare. Besides it was too late. He'd be long gone.

Caitlin opened the door with the chain in place. Standing there along with a bellboy and the luggage was the man who had caused her such grief. In spite of herself, her heart turned over.

"Please, Caitlin, let me in."

Anger surged through her. How dare he play out this miserable scene with an audience.

"Caitlin," Jake pleaded. "I need to talk to you. I'm in...pain." And holding up his right hand, shoved it through the space in the door. The hand was in a cast, swathed in bandages.

"See a doctor," she said inanely, all too aware of the bellboy's interest.

"Please, Caitlin. There's not another place in town to stay. I promise I won't bother you. Just for tonight?"

Pride fought with compassion. She'd always been a sucker. He deserved nothing. Her glance took in the drawn face, the tired eyes. Slowly she unlatched the chain, waited impassively as the bellboy brought in the luggage, and Jake pulled a bill from his pocket with his good hand and gave it to him.

The door closed, and they were left alone facing each other. He held up the cast. "The old break. I did it again, hitting him."

"Serves you right."

"It hurts like hell," he muttered. "I spent hours waiting in the emergency room." Caitlin watched him as he struggled with his jacket and accidentally hit the injured hand against a table. He groaned, and she winced.

"Didn't the doctor give you any painkiller?"She made sure her voice was cold.

"Some codeine. I had the cab stop at the liquor store in town. This will work better." Awkwardly. he pulled a pint of brandy from his jacket pocket and put it on the table.

Jake began to struggle to get the jacket off. Caitlin watched as long as she could stand it and then muttered. "Do it this way," and she eased his coat off.

Jake looked terrible. He had borrowed a razor that morning from Signore Basciani, but a faint stubble was beginning to appear. The expensive clothes were wrinkled worse than before, his eyes glazed with fatigue and pain.

Jake sat down on the couch, untied his shoes with his good hand and slipped them off. "I'll just put my head down here."

"You can't sleep there. You'll keep hitting your hand. In here." She moved toward the bedroom.

"I'm not going to take your bed."

"It's not your decision to make." One hand under his elbow, she propelled him into the bedroom and flipped back the covers of the bed.

Jake tried undoing the buttons of the shirt with his left hand, but failed. Caitlin brushed his hand aside to get him out of it. Underneath was a warm, bare chest. Her breath came faster, but she wadded the shirt and threw it on a chair and reached for his belt.

She stopped, her face heated. Jake's voice was tired, but amused. "If you haven't seen a man in his undershorts by now, Caitlin, it's time you did."

She shot daggers at him, came back and undid the belt from the loop, yanking it back so far that he yelped.

"You'd better keep quiet," she warned. I'm one of those soft-headed people who can't walk past a sick dog. But if you know what's good for you, you'll keep your mouth closed.

Roughly, she pulled at the zipper and shucked off his pants, throwing them after the shirt, then pushed him down onto the bed.

"I'll get you a glass for your *medicine*," she said curtly and went into the bathroom. In the mirror she stared at herself, not wanting to see what she knew was reflected there. She wanted her anger to burn hot and strong. It was the only protection she had.

Caitlin grabbed a washcloth, rinsed it in hot water and wrung it out, then grabbed a glass for the brandy. Back in the bedroom,

Jake was already lying down, a sheet covering him to the waist. Caitlin poured two fingers of brandy in the glass and handed it to him. She watched as he drank it and closed his eyes.

Jake looked awful, and she steeled herself against the wave of pity that washed over her. His eyes opened and he saw the washcloth. "

What's that for?"

"So you can wash your lying face," she said.

"Thanks, darlin'," he answered gravely, and in a welcome spurt of fresh anger she threw it at him, hitting him squarely in the jaw.

"Caitlin," he protested in a weak voice. She went swiftly across the room to the door, slamming it behind her and sank down on the sofa.

Lord what a mess. She was still in love with him. Even knowing what kind of man he was. She shook her head. Gran had always said it, "No fool like a lovesick fool."

Caitlin waited until she thought the brandy had taken effect, then crept back through the bedroom to the bathroom. Jake's deep even breathing told her she'd have no further problem with him tonight. On her return, she grabbed her gown and robe from the suitcase.

In the living room she pulled out the sofa and sank down, putting in a restless night. Throughout the long hours, she made her plans. She would call for a plane reservation in the morning, go home to Hartford and then what?

Her brother Ken had often offered her a place to stay in California. She could close her shop and perhaps open one there. She loved the climate on the west coast. San Diego was almost like the Riviera.

She needed someplace far away where she could start a new life, where she could forget the years she'd wasted being engaged to Daniel and the farcical interlude with Jake. She wouldn't deny she loved him. But that didn't mean she had to suffer any longer than she already had.

Her mind made up, she fell into an uneasy sleep.

It was Caitlin who woke Jake the next morning. She had showered, dressed, gone down for coffee and come back to find him still in bed. She was closing her suitcase when he opened his eyes.

Jake pulled himself upright, giving her a view of the bare, muscled chest and dense stubble on his chin.

"Good God, I really slept." He stretched. "That brandy did the trick." He looked at her bending over the suitcase on the floor. "What are you doing?"

"Checkout is 1 p.m. I 'm going to the desk to see what the concierge has been able to do about getting me on a plane for home."

Jake pulled himself out of bed, unmindful of his boxers. "Let me shower and dress before you go down. Please," he urged when she turned an unsmiling face toward him. "I have something to say. Give me that courtesy at least. I know you think I don't deserve it, Caitlin. But I'm asking anyway," he added in a low voice.

Caitlin paused, then got up and went into the other room. In a moment she heard the shower. She saw him come out with a towel wrapped around him and try unsuccessfully to open his suitcase. She did it for him, steeling herself against the picture he made.

He disappeared, came back dressed in slacks and a polo shirt that matched the sapphire eyes, looking much like himself, thanks to an electric razor. Assured, neat, confident—and devastatingly good looking.

Jake sat down next to her on the sofa, put out a restraining hand when she tried to get up. He lifted his hand when she moved away from him. "I won't touch you. Please just listen for a moment."

Caitlin, don't let me spoil the rest of the trip," he began. "Drive us to Stresa. You can't miss Lake Maggiore. Some think it's the most beautiful part of the Lake District. You'll be able to get a train back to Milan at the end of your stay. It will make me feel better if you finish out your trip and not cut it short. I've a business acquaintance in Stresa who will help me get the car back to Rome."

"I'm not interested in making you feel better…"

"Then do it for your own sake. Why would you throw away several days you could be spending in a wonderful spot."

Because, she wanted to tell him, because Jake Riordan had already spoiled them. But even as she formed the thought she was wavering, knowing full well that to extend her torment was madness. Still… What a masochist she was!

Chapter 14

The hotel in Stresa fronted on the glittering, sun-lit Lago Maggiore, offering an unparalleled view of Isola Pescatori and Isola Bella in the middle. The miniature islands with their ornamental gardens were breathtaking. Above the blue waters, the snow-crested Alps soared and pierced the clouds.

The bellboy had followed Caitlin to the suite with her luggage while Jake had telephoned his friend from the lobby. She looked around. The suite was one very large open room. It featured a sitting room at one end with views of the lake and at the other a huge bed on a slight platform. The hotel was fairly new, the furnishings a blend of traditional and modern in colors reflecting the mountains and lake.

Caitlin had left the door unlatched. In a few moments Jake came through, a bellboy depositing his luggage just inside the door. She waited until the man left then gave Jake a long look, her gaze stopping briefly on the luggage.

"Don't tell me. Let me guess. The business acquaintance is away for the holidays."

Jake looked at her, said nothing. Except for the cast, he was himself, no trace of fatigue.

Caitlin sucked in her breath, went on in a strained voice. "No, actually, there is no business acquaintance in Stresa. You made him up. Isn't that true?"

Still he said nothing. Caitlin, her temper rising, moved toward him. "What's the matter? Don't tell me your lies are beginning to stick in your throat?"

She laughed, a brittle sound. "Don't worry about it. You do it so well, Jake. Lie, that is. And your lies all fit together so neatly. Who Jake Riordan is, your reason for showing up in Portofino, your fiancée..." She laughed again, but this time the sound broke in the middle, sounding suspiciously like a sob.

"Caitlin!" She turned away, started walking toward the balcony. He caught her in mid-step with his good hand, turned her toward him, keeping a firm grip on her arm.

She looked at him with an imploring gaze. "Why, Jake? Why don't you just leave? What more do you want from me? What made you come here to Stresa?"

He swore softly. "You know the answer."

She looked over at the bed. "So you could finish what you started." She wrenched away from him, walked across the room to the bed, stepped up on the platform.

"Well, if that's all it takes to get you out my life, let's get it over with." She kicked off her shoes, put her hand on the top button of the dress, undid it, started on the next.

"Stop that!" Jake moved across the room, pushing her hand away. "You've got to listen to me, Caitlin."

"I don't have to listen to anything. Not from you."

Gently, Jake pushed her down to sit on the bed, then sat beside her. "No more lies, Caitlin. No evasions. The truth. Now and forever."

"Oh, yes," she drawled and made a mocking face.

Jake scowled. "You do that one more time and you're asking for trouble," he said. "You've got it coming, anyway, for not letting me explain yesterday on the terrace. And," the sapphire eyes gleamed dangerously, "for hitting me in the face with a wet washcloth last night."

"Explain? Oh, you explained."

"I'm warning you, Caitlin." There was a ragged edge to his voice, and his grip tightened, preventing her from moving.

She sat still, angry, but unable to keep from breathing in the scent of him, his presence as heady as ever.

"Let's get one thing straight," Jake began. "Yes, I want you. Oh, how I want you. I came here to Stresa with the specific intent of making love to you."

Caitlin drew in her breath, but Jake was still talking. "But that was only one of my objectives and far from the most important. As wonderful and delightful as it promises to be, there are several items which are more important."

Caitlin looked up at him, said tremulously, "Which are?"

170

"In order of importance?"

"Yes." Her voice was hoarse, her need to believe never greater.

"There are two that are foremost. They're of equal significance."

"Go on."

His voice was still frayed. "To make you understand why I did and said what I did. The other: convincing you that I love you and will love you until the end of my days."

Caitlin sat very still, the fire that was kindling within her licking at the cold numbness around her heart "What else?"

"Making you promise to marry me. Here in Italy. As soon as possible. Before we go home."

Jake drew a deep breath, and continued. "At first, I thought it necessary we go home first, so we could see Daniel and explain. Daniel was my friend. I couldn't just take his girl. But he didn't deserve you, and you didn't love him. You sent him packing. I heard you."

Her head jerked up, heat replacing the cold paralysis. "I sent you packing, too," she said her heart clamoring within her chest.

"I don't always do what I'm told," he said softly. "Especially when the stakes are so high." His good hand reached up to stroke her hair. "There was no way on earth I was going to let you get away from me. Especially after you told me you loved me back there on the mountain."

"But why did you lie to me? Caitlin cried out and rose to look at him straight on, moving out of his reach when he tried to grab her. "About Jenny, about knowing Daniel?"

"Would you have come with me if you'd known I was there on Daniel's behalf?"

Caitlin stood unmoving, and after a long pause, shook her head.

"Telling you that Jenny was my girl was stupid. She's been Harry's intended since they were kids. She delayed their wedding until her father remarries which is soon. She didn't want him to be alone."

Jake continued. "I thought it would make you feel safe with me. I wanted you to think I wasn't attracted to you." He laughed softly. "I don't think I succeeded. Do you know what an effort it was to keep from making love to you? I was a crazy man…"

Caitlin looked at him, hesitant, the ice cracking and melting inside, leaving a puddle of emotion. She was drowning in the sapphire gaze.

Jake searched her face. "Caitlin," he said softly. "Do you believe me? Do you know how much I love you?"

She bit her lower lip, nodded, said in a low voice, "Oh, Jake. I can't help it. I love you, too."

He let out a deep breath, his gaze inflaming her, and in seconds they were clinging to one another, the sob in her throat muted by his mouth.

Caitlin tightened her hold on him as he swung her gently onto his lap, smoothing her hair, caressing her face, murmuring endearments.

After a while he lifted his head, and said, "I called Paolo just now, down in the lobby."

"You did? Why? About the car?"

Jake shook his head. "To see if he can pull some strings, if necessary. He can. We'll be married in Rome. If that's all right with you. I'm taking no chances. You're mine and I want the world to know it."

"You mean it?"

"I've meant it all along." Jake's voice softened. "Since that moment I saw you standing there in that bit of silk on the balcony at the Fiorito. You blew me away. Wait, you'll see…" He left her for a moment to go to his luggage. "You packed this suitcase. I can't believe you didn't see it."

He handed her a miniature velvet cube. Caitlin opened it. The sapphire and diamond ring she had admired in the window at Lugano winked up at here. She let out a cry.

"You bought this? That day in Lugano. When you were being so mean to me?"

"You said you loved it. That it was simple but elegant. But if you've changed your mind and want something different…."

How could she when this would remind her forever of the sea as a backdrop in their travels.

Caitlin let Jake slip it on her finger. The band fit perfectly. She pressed her mouth to the sapphire winking up at her, then to his hand and to his mouth in a quick kiss.

` "It's the most beautiful thing I've ever seen in my life. I was afraid you were buying it for Jenny. That you were going to honeymoon with her at the Villa d'Este."

Jake laughed out loud. "Sapphires are too tame for Jenny. Her taste runs to the ultra modern—twisted silver and black opals. And I'll stay at the Villa d'Este with no one but you. I made it clear to Daniel before he left that you were mine." He hauled her back into his lap as if to emphasize possession.

Jake's mouth, firm and urgent, covered hers. "We've so many things to talk about, to decide. Do you want to honeymoon right away or go home and meet each other's families first? Bibi will be ecstatic. Getting *two* daughters! I really want us to be married now," Jake said, "but if you…'

Caitlin put a finger over his mouth. "So do I. Then I want to take you home and introduce you to my family, especially to Gran…" She broke off, laughing. "She'll be so proud of you-- hitting Daniel for saying those awful things." She took his injured hand and kissed the tips of the fingers that showed through the cast. "Are you sure you're all right?"

"I'm fine, not hampered at all." He pushed her back onto the bed to nuzzle her throat.

"But will you be able to …"

"Love you properly?" he finished for her, laughing tenderly as soft color rushed into her face. "You've no worries on that score. I intend to be the consummate lover…a devoted husband…an exemplary father."

"That's not what I was going to ask," she protested, her arms tightening around him. She stretched to kiss his ear, the only place she could reach in his stranglehold, trying to remember just what she had been going to ask him. Something about driving the car back to Rome…

Then the rest of his words sank in, driving all other thoughts from her head. "You do?" she said dreamily.

His good hand, suddenly nimble, undid another button to demonstrate his dexterity.

"Yup," Jake said in his best cowboy voice. "I do."

The End

If you enjoyed this story about Caitlin and Jake please consider leaving a review on Amazon.com and be sure to check out other Stone Pine titles.

Patricia Costa Viglucci Books
Readers' Comments

Pride and Pretense—*Great romance! Steamy and sweet*

Jordan's Island-- *Intriguing storyline… Super enjoyable…My kind of romance*

The Connecticut Cowboy and the Runaway Bride--*Loved the Riviera setting and the delightful characters*

The Troubleman Takes a Wife—*Sizzles, great story and characters*

Growing Up Italian in God's Country—*Kudos for a meticulous, masterful family memoir.*

Sun Dance at Turtle Rock, YA--*Fast paced, greatly enjoyed it.*

Beware the Ghost Riders, YA mystery—I'd give this book more than five stars if I could!

Cassandra Robbins, Esq., YA—*Coming of age romance. Couldn't put it down.'*

Don't Kiss Me Goodbye! *A companion to Growing Up Italian*

Also from Stone Pine Books

Albany Street Kid—A Look Back at the 40s by *Carmen J. Viglucci---Master story teller*

The East Fork Revisited: a memoir *by Alfred F. Borelli,*
Growing up in the Allegheny Mountains in the '30s--humor abounds.

.